KŌHINE

KŌHINE

COLLEEN MARIA LENIHAN

First published in 2022 by Huia Publishers
39 Pipitea Street, PO Box 12280
Wellington, Aotearoa New Zealand
www.huia.co.nz

ISBN 978-1-77550-697-3

Copyright © Colleen Maria Lenihan 2022

Front Cover:
Portrait photography copyright © Colleen Maria Lenihan 2022
City photograph courtesy Greg Jeanneau/Unsplash.com

Interior photography copyright © Colleen Maria Lenihan 2022
Back cover city photography courtesy of Orlie K/Unsplash.com

This book is copyright. Apart from fair dealing for the purpose of private study, research, criticism or review, as permitted under the Copyright Act, no part may be reproduced by any process without the prior permission of the publisher.

A catalogue record for this book is available from the National Library of New Zealand.

Published with the support of the

for Monique

E kore au e ngaro
he kākano i ruia mai
i Rangiātea

CONTENTS

1	Gnossienne No. 1
9	Cherry Blossom Girl
21	Ruru
31	Nerissa
41	Little Miss Paranoid
49	Paradise
61	Autumn Feeling
69	Spirit House
79	Idol
89	Love Hotel
97	The Storm
111	Mama
119	Leaping-off Place I
131	The Void
137	Just Holden Together
147	Private Dancer
157	Directions
165	Pepe Tuna
177	Sushi Train
183	Tama
191	The Actor
213	Sista
215	Leaping-off Place II
219	Acknowledgements

Gnossienne No. 1

Slabs of sunlight fall, dust motes float like amoeba across the room. Books, sheet music and vinyl records line the walls, cover the tatami in wooden cases and teeter in precarious stacks. In the tokonoma, a pair of hand-tinted photographs hang above a black lacquer shrine.

Yuki is playing a sensual, jazzy arrangement. It is only her second attempt, so you feel good-natured and forbearing about her fumbles on the keys. Finally, she gets a feel for the piece. She closes her eyes like a torch singer and launches into the chorus, her surprisingly husky voice plaintive.

You usually detest J-pop, but you have to admit this piece by Nakashima Mika is quite charming. You have been teaching Yuki piano since she was ten, when her family first moved to Tokyo. Her mother called on you with a gift of green tea from Kyoto, saying she'd heard you were the best piano teacher in Shibuya-ku and would you please look upon her favourably and take her Yuki on?

The winter sun rings Yuki's glossy black bob; her shoulders rise and fall. As always, she is in school uniform: white blouse, check skirt fashionably shortened, baggy white socks. She sings the last line, which pleads in English:

'Please ... please ...'

The notes hang in the air. You walk over to her, clapping.

'Subarashii, Yuki-chan.'

She shakes her head.

'Ie, ie, Hamasaki-sensei. So many mistakes.'

'Such feeling though.'

'My best friend sings this at karaoke. She lives in your building.'

Yuki slings her schoolbag over her shoulder, bows and says goodbye. As she walks out the door, you take in her long Bambi legs, the swing of her hips ... this is a young girl about to blossom. You feel pangs of moe. Not in a lecherous way. More a protective wonder.

Gnossienne No. 1

The 'Super View' Odoriko train looks like a Shinkansen but has wider windows and moves at a far more leisurely pace. Sitting on the left for the views of the Pacific below, you see the island of Ōshima in the distance. Your surfboard has been sent ahead to the guesthouse you always stay at in Shimoda. A full wetsuit with booties and a hood is packed in your canvas duffle bag, ready for the chilly typhoon swells due to roll in from the north-east. The train attendant rattles past with her cart. You order a Kirin beer to have with the bento box you purchased at the station. Shōgayaki is your favourite, and you devour the juicy slices of pork. The family seated in front of you are at the window. The father points out the fishing boats to his little girl. Her chubby hand traces circles in the air. You think about Natalie, the woman who had once loved you, and imagine what you'd say to her if she was sitting next to you in the first-class car.

'What's the most beautiful thing you've ever seen?'

You already knew your answer. A volcano erupting in Hawai'i. Natalie, with the heart-shaped face and cropped blonde hair, would think for a second, then say:

'You.'

A cab deposits you outside a white weatherboard guest-house. There are two houses side by side and double storeyed: four units. A faded sign says 'AZUL BEACH SIDE

CONDOMINIUM'. The owner, Abe-san, an old surfer in worn tie-dye and camo Crocs, greets you. He gives you the key to your usual room on the second floor, the one with the framed print of the Matterhorn. Your surfboard is waiting for you at the door. You remember when Natalie kicked off her Mary-Janes and rushed in to jump up and down on the bed like a child. You'd joined her, until you both fell back on the pillows, breathless.

You fix yourself a Jack and Coke and smoke on the balcony until dark.

The next day you are up early at what Natalie used to call 'Dawn's crack'. You had hoped dating an Australian would improve your English, but it's mada sugoku heta. You brew coffee and drink it on the balcony. Your eyes scan the swell. In the half-light, sand, sky and sea are strips of texture, like a grainy black-and-white photo.

The beach is deserted. It is closed at this time of year. You are breaking the rules, but the locals don't care about the few die-hard surfers like yourself who still head out in winter. Izu people are relaxed like that. It is a relief to be out of Tokyo, away from the sea of people and crushing weight of collective obligation. You amble onto the beach with your board and take in long, deep breaths. The sky is bone white and the ocean is grey. The spare desolation exhilarates you, and you break into a jog. The freezing water shocks you awake. You must keep moving so the cold doesn't overtake your senses and force you back to shore. You jump on the board and paddle out.

Flat water. A lull. Out there amongst it all, you are totally alone. Scraps of fog cling to the ragged coast behind you, and you catch spooky, sharky feelings. You negotiate with the ocean: don't drown me, or give me a beating. I don't need any trouble. Black lumps form in the distance. You paddle up and down the beach, in search of the perfect position to catch a wave when the set rolls in.

You sigh as you ease yourself into the steaming waters of the onsen. For a moment you are the luckiest man in the world. Eyeing the 'TATTOOS PROHIBITED' sign, you drape a wash cloth over yourself to conceal the tiny inking on your inner forearm. You and Natalie had got each other's initials on a bender in Thailand. The next day, she'd laughed and said, 'Winona Forever!' She made you want to be gaijin too sometimes. You wouldn't have to think so much before you opened your mouth. You wish she was up to her pale neck in the cypress tub with you, green eyes shining. They changed colour according to the weather and her mood. The opalescent chalkiness of the mineral pool would probably make them a light grey green. Where is she? What is she doing now? She who was once the centre of your life is now an unknowable stranger. You resolve to banish Natalie from your mind, once and for all. You block her on every platform and delete all evidence of the relationship from your phone.

The routine for the next four days is this: up at Dawn's crack, coffee and cigarette, surf until your teeth chatter, soak in healing waters, fall asleep in massage chair, pad back to your room in yukata and slippers, re-read Murakami's *Norwegian Wood*, drink Jakku Coku on the deck until midnight.

* * *

You catch the train back to Tokyo, hungry for your favourite ramen, icy cold pints at your local izakaya, your piano. You look forward to seeing your students and asking them about their holidays. You alight at Daikanyama Station. It's nice out. Young fashionable couples stroll past looking pleased with themselves and their choices. They throng the outdoor café. You smile at a black French bulldog being pushed around in a buggy. It smiles back. Your apartment block is nearby, just a minute away. You stop by Lawson's to get a tamago sando and a can of hot Royal Milk Tea. A handwritten note is taped to your door.

Gnossienne No. 1

Hamasaki-san
Please contact Shibuya Police Station
03-3498-0110

Huh? You read it again. Your heart starts to pound. You grab the note, unlock the door, dump your bag in the genkan. Have you been robbed? No broken windows. You scan for signs of a break-in, but your stacks and piles appear undisturbed. You dial the number on the note, and a woman puts you through to a Detective Furiyama.

'On January first, a gaijin living on the fourth floor of your building, Daikanyama Royal Copo, jumped from their balcony and landed in your backyard. Police and ambulance workers had to enter while you were away. We are sorry for the trouble.'

'Eh! Hontō desu ka? Are they okay?'

'She died. A high school student. It is most regrettable.'

You hang up. Your hands tremble as you light a cigarette. You look upon the picture of your grandmother; an attempt to draw comfort from her serene countenance. You step into the yard and see the wooden fence has been knocked askew. A crow has lit on it, so black it is almost blue. It watches as you see the blood on the concrete tiles. You look up to see the balcony the girl jumped from. It's higher than you expect.

You light several sticks of incense with your grandfather's silver Zippo. Thick white smoke curls up into the cold January air, releasing agarwood and benzoin. Press your palms together and bow. You think of this girl and her parents. You think of your parents. You think of their parents. You think of your childhood pet, Mochi. You think of Kano-sensei, your piano teacher. You think of your student, Yuki-chan. You think of Natalie.

The incense clings to your clothes and follows you inside. You search through the piles of sheet music to find a piece by Satie and sit down at the piano. His unusual notation instructs you to perform 'monotonously and whitely', 'very shiningly' and 'from afar'. You play and the melody slips out of the room into the yard, whirls for a while with the drifts of smoke, and then floats up, up, up into the ether.

Cherry Blossom Girl

At 5 a.m., a phone call:

'Where are you?'

The taxi came to a halt outside the Shibuya Police Station. Maia noticed what a lovely morning it was. Crisp blue skies, everything blanketed in snow. New Year's Day was always the quietest day of the year in Tokyo.

She ran into the police station, footsteps clattering in the hush, to an elevator that took her underground to a room at the end of a dim corridor, and there in the gloom, three policemen bowed deeply to a form draped in white. She pulled back the sheet. The tongue protruded slightly, bitten hard with even white teeth. Maia clung to Aria and felt how cold she was, small breasts like stones against her chest. Sixteen years old, forever. Her knees gave way, and one of the cops began to weep.

Maia set to the task of ringing people around the world and ruining their New Year.

'My poor mother,' she said after the most difficult phone call.

'Poor Maia,' said Hiromi, perched at the foot of Maia's bed.

Maia drank cans of beer and shook under the covers. She stared at Aria's picture on her gaijin card. Dark eyes gazed back at her with an amused air, like she was about to say something funny.

In the night, remnants of Maia's Catholic upbringing kicked in. She recited the Angelus, Hail Marys over and over, like a rosary.

'Holy Mary, Mother of God, pray for us sinners, now and at the hour of our death. Amen.'

Hiromi drove Maia out to the funeral home on the outskirts of the city. A fleet of hearses were parked outside with ornate shrines grafted on to their roofs. They looked like mobile Buddhist temples. Staff in black wore ashy make-up, which made them look dead themselves. Hiromi dealt with the funeral director, who constantly mopped his brow and sucked air through his teeth. The death of a foreigner was a lot of trouble, especially at this time of year. With a pained expression, he insisted that Maia view the body before they undertook any embalming.

'No, I will do it,' said Hiromi, reasoning that Maia shouldn't see Aria again until she was surrounded by her family in New Zealand. Maia didn't know what was best. The logistics of repatriating a body were overwhelming. There were so many decisions.

Hiromi came back to the car afterwards, green from the smell of formaldehyde.

'They dressed Aria in a beautiful kimono,' she said, and touched Maia lightly on the arm before turning to throw up on the edge of the carpark.

Maia carefully placed the framed photograph that she had been clutching to her chest like a lifebuoy in the seat pocket in front of her so that Aria was facing out. *Please don't anyone speak to me.* The instant the thought arose, the woman sitting next to her said, 'Who is that? She is very pretty.'

'My daughter,' Maia said.

'Where is she?'

'She's on the plane.'

'But why isn't she sitting with you?'

'She's in the cargo hold.'

The long wooden box was lifted out gently and greeted by booming voices and the stamping of feet across the tarmac. It was morning. Airport workers stood by and watched the fierce haka in silence.

Exhausted, Maia collected her baggage and cleared customs. Sleep, when she could get it, was a brief reprieve, but each time she woke up she had to realise all over again that Aria was gone, forever. It was like standing in a field of shattered glass, shards stuck upright into the earth in all directions, as far as the eye could see.

Her brother was waiting for her in the arrivals hall. They embraced. She stepped back and took a good look at him. She hadn't seen Tāne in years. His fine features were wreathed in lines.

'You look old,' she said.

They walked out to his car without speaking. As the V8 engine sputtered into a loud, low rumble, she lit a cigarette and looked out the window. Patches of scrubby vegetation under a colourless sky.

They arrived to whānau waiting outside the house in light drizzle. A long line of people to hongi and kiss and hug. Maia sat next to Aria on a mattress. At night, someone strummed a guitar and quietly sang. An old friend rushed up and held Maia very, very tight. Countless kids. Maia struggled to identify them, and occasionally would grab one for a cuddle, and ask: 'Who's your mother?'

'Aunty, is that your daughter, eh? Did she fall down?' a child said, as she gazed at Aria's body in her coffin.

Big pots of boil-up and fried bread. Cousins in the kitchen. Flowers and messages, even a dozen bottles of good vodka. *I can use those*, thought Maia. A cloak of kiwi feathers on the coffin, so precious that it must always be accompanied by a caretaker. Photographs of ancestors displayed and spoken to as if they were alive. Karakia in the mornings and at night. Unearthly wailing as the lid was put on the coffin and screwed firmly shut.

The service. Photo slideshow, a life in review. Here she is as a toddler, wearing the plastic gold medals around her neck that she'd loved – Aria, the Champion of the World. Next, a middle-schooler flashing the V sign with her friends at Tokyo Disneyland. Now coltish and doe-eyed, heavy eyeliner accentuating those anime eyes, posing in Hachikō Square. A J-pop song played as the images flashed past.

The burial.

'Put all your mamae in there with her,' said a woman whom Maia didn't know.

Spades dug furiously; blades glinted in the sunshine. Gosh they filled that hole up quick. Her brother's hand heavy on her back. The sun beat down on them.

Outside the floor-to-ceiling glass, Mount Fuji stood sentinel above stacks of gleaming towers. Maia never thought she'd feel relieved to be back in the office, but the calm pervading the Japanese law firm as attorneys and their secretaries quietly went about their work was a salve. She'd used up all her meagre annual leave in January for the tangi. A full year of work stretching ahead with no holidays was daunting, but she couldn't think about that now.

Her office was filled with sunlight. She closed the door, took a breath and set to organising her desk. There was a knock. Her boss, a kindly older English man, stood at the door. She nodded. After an awkward moment, he said, 'Come here,' and gave her a quick clumsy hug, which made her tear up.

'What should I say if the lawyers ask how my New Year was?'

'Don't tell them. It'll be easier for you if they don't know.'

Maia's ex-husband rang while she was eating a bento at her desk.

'I saw her,' said Dai. 'You know I don't believe in this stuff. But *I know* it was her.'

Aria had come to him in a dream. Walking down Meiji Dori near their old house, eight years old, the age she'd been when she first came to Japan.

'She doesn't know she's dead yet, but she's okay.'

Aria's best friend, Yuki, dreamed that Aria was building a house for her and her boyfriend in New Zealand.

'Tell Masaya to stop crying,' Aria had said.

Tāne had dreamt of her too, which frightened him because Aria asked him to join her.

Maia dreamed of transporting Japanese kokeshi dolls in wooden boxes by bus and being engulfed by wave upon wave of tsunami, but never once of Aria.

Trudging up the hill to catch the train home after work, Maia passed through Roppongi Crossing with all its neon enticements, hostesses and strippers in full hair and make-up hurrying to dates with their customers, touts lying in wait. How was it she was still here? Snatches of Townes Van Zandt songs played on an endless loop in her mind. The master of despair had died on New Year's Day too, which gave her a strange kind of solace.

It was as if someone had taken a giant roller of paint and covered Maia completely in grey. All she wanted to do was assume the fetal position somewhere dark and quiet, but the pressing need to make a living forced her to maintain the pretence that she wasn't a shell of a human, a mere placeholder where the person Maia used to be. Her students were lawyers and worked extremely long hours, and like all Japanese, were conditioned to be stoic and to never complain. Yet Maia was one of those people who others felt comfortable telling things to. Many of her students had opened up about their daily worries and concerns, their deepest darkest secrets. Before Aria's death, she had been happy to listen.

One afternoon, Hama-sensei, a sweet but naive woman in her late twenties, had complained about the other lawyer in her office. Whenever he was finished with a phone call, he would slam the receiver down, startling her.

'He put the phone down like this, gachan!' she'd said, and demonstrated the action like a karate chop. This had been going on for months and was driving Hama-sensei mad. Maia's suggestion to politely ask her colleague to stop doing this was met with wide-eyed scepticism. The other lawyer was her senpai, her senior, and Hama-sensei said that it was impossible to ask him to do anything of the sort without causing deep offence.

'It's a big problem, isn't it?' Hama-sensei said.

You think that's a big problem? Maia wanted to say. Try repatriating your child's body.

Trudging up the hill to the station after work, Maia cried every day.

Maia made three piles: keep, donate, discard. The keep pile was the biggest. She couldn't bring herself to get rid of Aria's school uniform, the battered copy of *How Maui Found His Mother*, the purple Thai Airways blanket that Aria had stolen on their trip to Koh Phi Phi. She couldn't keep all of Aria's school books, so she went through and cut out every single place she'd written her name, and put the slivers of paper in a lacquer box. She found a list that Aria had written of the things that she'd wanted to be when she grew up: make-up artist, DJ, stylist. DJ took her by surprise. Dai was a DJ, and on learning that Maia's current boyfriend was a DJ as well, Aria had declared them to be losers.

A pink plastic hair comb, a single, long, dark brown hair tangled in its teeth. Maia turned it over again and again in her hand. A piece of worthless junk, yet here it was, existing.

Daily routine really started to get to her. Hell, the whole world got to her.

The Hibiya Line, packed on a Thursday morning. Bleary-eyed salarymen clutched their briefcases and nursed hangovers. An office girl, immaculately presented in stockings and tweed suit, constantly nodded off and rested her head on a stranger's shoulder for a split second before jerking her head upright over and over, never once fully awakening. A group of high-school girls in eye-wateringly short skirts, baggy jumpers and loose socks flipped their hair around and looked at their phones. One, slender with long dark brown hair, slouched nonchalantly in a familiar and startling way. This happened occasionally; in crowds, on subway platforms, outside train stations. Maia's heart would leap into her throat.

The girl turned her head, and Maia saw that she had bad teeth. Not pretty after all, not beautiful like her, *not her*.

Why are *you* alive? she thought bitterly.

Maia couldn't sleep, again. She lay on her back on the hard sofa bed in the living room. Since Aria's death, she couldn't sleep in the room they had once shared in their tiny central Tokyo apartment. Television helped in the evenings, but she'd binge-watched everything, and now there was nothing to do but lie here and wait for the morning. Try not to look into the abyss. A black hole that she could only glance at, give the ole side eye, because she knew that if she were to look directly into it, she'd fall in and disappear. It took a lot of mental effort, this *not looking*. She was exhausted. Without the energy to toss and turn, her mind finally blank, she stared at the ceiling.

Then, she left her body.

* * *

Maia was floating in mid-air, just slightly above herself. Held gently in the palm of a giant invisible hand. A kind of forcefield. Energy emanated from her palms. There was no thought. Just being. She gazed at a vortex of violet swirling energy directly above her forehead for a long, suspended moment. Was it minutes, or hours? There was no time. She could have stayed there forever.

** * ***

The phone rang and rang, its shrill tones breaking the spell, and she was pulled back into her body with a snap. It took a few minutes for Maia to answer it, and her words tumbled out in a useless jumble. She hung up. In that moment, her grief was completely, utterly and entirely gone. She slept peacefully for the first time in almost a year.

Finally, Aria came to Maia in a dream. She was standing in a room filled with moonlight. With a cry, Maia swept Aria up in her arms.

'I love you, Aria,' she said. 'You know that, right?'

Aria didn't hug her back, but Maia could feel her smile against her shoulder.

'Mum, *I know*,' she said. Sixteen years old, forever. 'Can I go back upstairs now?'

Ruru

I had come to the barbeque with Ben, but a few glasses of pinot gris later, I decided I actually preferred the host, Tim. As Ben drove off, Tim's hand slipped inside my underwear. We fooled around a bit. Danced to eighties' music on the deck. Told him my Axl Rose story and he laughed. Told him of my great loss and he cried. We had the idea to go for a swim, and he drove us dead drunk down to the beach. Lost the car keys on the sand in the dark, and Tim had to ask strangers for help. We used the light of their cellphones.

'Is that girl naked?' I heard one say.

Back at the house, the ruru came. It perched on the railing of the deck and its shining eyes stared like a tekoteko, golden pools that hinted at an awareness of secrets and sacred things. I knew that the ruru had come because I was there, my first night at Te Henga.

'Can I live here?' I asked Tim.

'Yes,' he said.

I did wonder, for a second, what kind of person would let a stranger move in after a drunken hook-up, but I figured someone kind of crazy, like me.

The call of the ruru haunted me, most evenings after sunset. It lived in a dead tree at the rear of the house, which was hollow and had a large entrance, so the ruru could pitch straight into its nest with spread wings. Or so I imagined. Later, I mentioned the ruru to my aunty, who said, 'I would have left straight away.'

But its visit was a good sign. I was so happy there. When I walked down the track through native bush to the dunes, fantails would follow and dance around my path, their fans like miniature taiaha. Every night I would wake at three in the morning and listen to the forest breathe. My new bedroom looked out into an amphitheatre of nīkau, which in the moonlight became sinewy figures, arms raised high.

'You're always awake,' Tim said.

I winked at him.

'If you snooze, you lose.'

'Shall we go for a picnic?' Tim said, and with a tartan blanket and transistor radio, we set out to find a good spot to eat crackers and drink wine. Our favourite place overlooked a crescent-shaped bay, on a hillside planted with gold flax. We talked of Te Kawerau ā Maki, the tribe who had once lived here, and tried to identify their pā sites.

'You don't seem like a Pākehā,' I said.

'Chur, my Māori,' he said, and I laughed and kissed his face.

His arms were tattooed and muscular and he had strong, brown hands. I liked to look at them while he was driving, shucking mussels, building things. I thought about how his hands would feel on my body, later, in the bed that he'd elevated to take full advantage of the panorama laid out before us: rugged Bethells Beach to the west, and, inland, black sand dunes that you could trek across to Lake Wainamu in the east. Tim's room was on the top floor of the round house. Festooned with flags, it reminded me of the crow's nest in a pirate ship. I lay on his bed in lingerie and stilettos, and waited for him to return from the city.

'I love coming home,' he said.

He was so active. I took a lot of photographs of the back of him, as I was always trying to keep up; through the bush, over the dunes, and down the beach. There are no pictures of us together from that time. A pity, that.

Gliding through the house that summer, I felt elated. This place gave me refuge. I needed it. Here the days were full of possibility, and the twilight skies were rosé pink.

I began making a Māori birdman kite out of toetoe from the dunes and raupō that I collected from the creek at the bottom of the track. While saying karakia and hauling bundles of raupō up the muddy track, I liked to think that the ancestors of Te Kawerau ā Maki were looking upon me with approval. I made the frame from the kākaho, and bound them together with strips of harakeke, the neat little Xs reminiscent of tukutuku panels. I lashed varying lengths of mauve, grey and brown raupō to the body and wings. I kept thinking of a friend who had died. I had not thought of him for many years. He'd gassed himself in his car. His name was Kahurangi, but everyone called him Blue. Maybe I could name the kite after him so when I eventually flew it, it would somehow reactivate his mauri, setting it free, high in the sky above the black sand dunes.

The creek was swollen with rain. Tim and I were on our way to the lake, following the track next to the creek. I stopped to take photos of the light dancing off the water, which created glowing orbs of bokeh between the wide banks of the sandy riverbed.

We sat for a while in silence, sunning ourselves. A cabbage tree was in flower, the fragrant clusters of tiny white flowers attracting bees. The floral sprays nestled amongst the spiky leaves gave the tree a sparky aliveness.

This fine tree deserves a better name than cabbage tree, I thought.

Its leaves vibrated with agreement.

I'll stick to tī kōuka from now on, I said silently to the tree. It suits you better.

After a spell, Tim stood up all creaky.

'You're like the tin man,' I said.

He kicked me and I laughed.

'What's he lacking again? A brain?' I said.

'A heart, dummy.'

We traversed the sea of hot black sand and climbed a series of steep sand dunes. At the top of the last dune, the lake appeared like an oasis, a mirror for the green hillside and cloudless blue sky. The idyllic setting was spoiled by a pile of beer bottles and plastic sheeting at the lake's edge, discarded after someone's attempts to slide down the dunes into the water.

My hands balled into fists. 'I hope their lives are just as messy.'

'That sounds like a mākutu,' said Tim. 'Mad Māori.'

'I hate people.'

'Probably just some young Westies. They don't care.'

I thought of the ruru, the kaitiaki of this place.

'We can't leave it like this.'

We gathered the trash and carried it home with us.

I felt like eating mussels, so we went to our secret place, a bay that could only be reached at low tide, around a steep, rocky point. Agile and unafraid, Tim reached the shore first. He watched as I cautiously made my way around the rocks as the surf pounded away below. I tried not to look unfit or clumsy, but I'd lived in big cities for too long. I could tell he wanted to laugh, but he didn't.

'You're nearly there,' he said.

The mussels were plentiful. I held open a flax kete for Tim to drop the mussels in as he prised them off the rocks. Occasionally a big wave would threaten to engulf us and we'd have to scramble out of the way.

We strolled down the beach. Ours were the only footprints in the glittering iron sand. I took a photo of our trail snaking across the beach. It was late afternoon and everything was gold.

'This is all yours,' I said, sweeping my arm across the cove. 'I hereby declare this place Timland.'

He laughed and pulled me in for a kiss.

We climbed up a grassy bank. At the top, someone had made a fire pit. There were stumps to sit on and a swing lashed to a tree in the surrounding thicket of twisted mānuka. The site was perfectly positioned to view the whole bay.

I unpacked our provisions while Tim fired up the gas burner. In a battered old pot, I sautéed crushed garlic in butter, added the mussels and fresh herbs, and poured in a couple of glugs of wine. Tim sparked up a joint and passed it to me. I sat back and marvelled at his tattoos. I had been indifferent to tattoos before, but now I loved to trace the blue ink on his body with my eyes. Praying hands clutched a rosary on his forearm. A tekoteko ran up his side, propping up his heart. Mexican catrinas adorned both shins, and fiery skulls stared out fiercely from his knees. Sometimes I wanted to get inside his skin and wear it. Like those Aztec priests I studied at art school. I wanted to love him to death.

We ate the sweet fleshy mussels and washed them down with the remainder of the wine.

'I like the orange ones best,' I said.

'They all taste the same,' said Tim.

'The females taste much better. I wish we could stay here forever,' I said.

Together we looked out over the view, and then we were startled out of our reverie by the cry of the ruru. It was odd to hear him out here by the ocean, while it was still light.

'The tide,' said Tim, and pointed to the water. Barely an hour had passed, but already the sea was creeping up the sand and threatening to cut us off at the point. We gathered our things and made our way back with woozy urgency. A channel we had easily crossed earlier was now waist deep with churning water. I regretted smoking that joint.

'I got you,' Tim said.

He took my hand and we waded across slowly, holding our bags above the water.

'That was a king tide,' said Tim. 'The highest tide – it coincides with the full moon. We could have been stranded.'

'I need to be more careful what I wish for,' I said.

The summer faded gradually, then left. I was unused to how cold it was in New Zealand houses. I often felt colder inside than out. My kite remained unfinished. It was May.

'I'll fly it at Matariki,' I said. I had big ideas of celebrating Māori New Year with a party and plenty of kai. The days and days of rain put a damper on that.

Had it always rained so much? I thought. I guess that's why it's all so bloody green.

Matariki came and went, and still the latticed framework of the kite lay there, unfinished.

'When's the launch date?' asked Tim.

I shrugged. The question dissolved any last shred of interest I had in the project.

I got lonely sometimes, while Tim was working in the city. I was bored, not having found my niche yet, in contrast to his days of purposeful grafting. Sometimes he would come home and I'd be tipsy, FaceTiming with other drunk friends around the world. He'd look at the empty bottles and turn the news on. I'd go outside and listen to music and chain-smoke. The question hung in the air: What have you been doing all day?

Tim sat hunched over his computer, eating corn chips and salsa without offering me any. Later, in the car, a chill emanated from him.

'Hey, can you talk to me?' I said.

'What do you want to talk about?'

At the party, I went outside to smoke. Looking in, I could see Sam stroking Evie's hair as they sat on the sofa. Tim sat at the table and nursed his beer. I couldn't catch his eye.

After dinner, we all had mushroom tea except for Tim. The foul-tasting brew made my mouth numb. Mildly tripping on the way home, I watched streetlights become starbursts that smashed across the windscreen, while Tim's silence took on the grand proportions of empty ballrooms. He went straight to bed and wrapped himself stiffly in blankets.

'I can't sleep. Can you hold me?'

'Have a bath,' he said, and turned away.

In the tub, I looked down at my body, my thighs iridescent in the bubbles. Usually I would only see where a bellyful of arms and legs had marred it, but that night I saw it was beautiful. I slept in my own room.

It was a full moon and very bright outside my window. I felt the trees could move at any second. A nīkau beckoned to me.

'Haere mai ki konei,' it said. 'Tērā ngā kanohi kua tīkona e Matariki.'

I got up and entered the night. The tall ferns had crowns of fresh fronds on their heads, and nodded under the weight of all that new life. The sound of approaching wings beat through the silence, and I felt a cool rush of air as the ruru swooped, and slashed my face with its talons.

Nerissa

Twenty years after the Greek ship *Nerissa* sank at the entrance to the Hokianga Harbour in 1928, eight lives lost to the deep, I was born. Due to the Māori proclivity at the time for naming babies after tragedies, I was christened Nerissa.

My mother was an excellent honky tonk piano player and a terrible drunk, and she made no bones about not wanting me.

'When you were a baby, I didn't give you the tit,' she slurred, wild-eyed from another night on the waipiro. 'I gave you water from the ditch. Straight from the side of the road.'

My grandparents took me in when I was five and raised me on their small dairy farm deep in the Hokianga, far from any sealed roads.

'Nerissa pisser!' the kids jeered, while a dark stain bloomed around me on the tattered cloth seat. I had wet myself on the school bus again. I turned my face to the dusty window. Māmā was waiting by the side of the road. She wore workmen's trousers and a blue gingham scarf tied under her tattooed chin. The bus came to a halt. I hobbled off it. Years later, a doctor in Auckland would ask if I'd been in a car accident, as my pelvis was so out of whack. If only.

Māmā dried me off without complaint and hoisted me on to her back for the long walk home. Every day she carried me home from the school bus and gave me a mirimiri, until I could walk again.

* * *

Māmā and Pāpā took me to the Courthouse at Rawene for a hearing about my custody. I have a photo from that day. It was my seventh birthday. I am wearing a hat, ribbons in my hair, a hopeful smile. My mother never came.

* * *

The creak of bed springs woke me. I peered out from beneath my faded feather quilt. It was still night. Māmā was sitting bolt upright in the old iron bed by the window. A rope of thick white hair hung down her back and shone in the light of the full moon. It illuminated everything: the rocking chair with its peeling green paint in the corner, the grandfather clock that no longer chimed, the walls papered with yellowing pages of the *Northern Advocate*. 'Did you know? To be a wife of Solomon you would need perfect teeth. Try Cole's Dental Cream.' 'Drought In Northland Worst For Years.' 'NAGASAKI IS BURNING LIKE A VOLCANO'. The war was long over, but Māmā and Pāpā were still deathly afraid. 'If the Japanese come, we will run up into the hills.'

My gaze settled on a long whisker on Māmā's chin that caught the moonlight and glowed in high relief against the bluish green spirals etched on her skin. I didn't want to look at her eyes. They'd be staring into nothing. Māmā was silent. She was talking to the spirits of the dead.

I clung to my doll, Kuini. She was a faceless bundle of rags and the only toy I had. I told her my secrets.

Outside it was very still. I could hear every rustle. The forest was waiting. Māmā got up, drew her shawl around her shoulders and entered the night. She went deep into the ngahere to gather rongoā while the moon was high.

It felt like no time at all before Māmā was shaking me awake for milking time. I put on the grey pinafore I wore every day except Sundays and pulled on my gumboots. No time for breakfast. The cream had to be ready for the milk truck to collect by 5 a.m. or else it would sour at the gate. We'd eat after mahi. Tin mugs of strong tea, parāoa takakau with dripping, perhaps some fruit preserves.

I trudged through the wet grass with Māmā and Pāpā to where our small herd of cows were waiting. They were always ready, stock-still, with doleful eyes. I felt sorry for the cows come weaning time. They would cry for weeks after their calves were taken away.

After the herd had given up their milk, Māmā and Pāpā poured it into the separator. I watched as the blades spun round and round. The rhythm of the machine and the scent of warm milk made me long to climb back into bed. Once all the cream had been siphoned off into shiny metal cans for the factory, we pulled the machine apart and scrubbed it down thoroughly. Pāpā always made sure we were meticulous about everything, but it was especially important today. It was inspection time.

The Pākehā man from the factory peered over his glasses and his clipboard.

'The cream is still low grade. No improvement from last year,' he said.

Mr Jessop had crepey skin and jerky movements. I stared at his shiny pink head. None of the men I knew were bald. Pāpā, my uncles, all the kaumātua on the marae had thick, full heads of hair.

Mr Jessop wrote down the price the factory would pay for our cream. Pāpā spoke little English, and couldn't understand how the Pākehā came up with his numbers. I didn't trust him. I was sure he was hoodwinking us.

That night as we warmed ourselves by the fire, Pāpā said, 'Who's sick?'

'They told me to see the Maxwell girl, and make a poultice of tūpākihi for her arm,' said Māmā. 'Lucky I did. She'd had a nasty fall. It was badly swollen.'

'Good,' Pāpā said. My grandparents only ever spoke of Māmā's night-time excursions between themselves by the fire at night. They were devout Catholics. The church would not approve of such things.

'Get the horses, girl,' Māmā said. I went down to the paddock bearing carrots and caught the horses. We rode down the peninsula bareback. We dismounted and sat on a grassy bank that overlooked the harbour for a while, and then Māmā slowly gathered herself up. She seemed to unfold and expand herself, until she was standing. She appeared even taller, somehow. Eyes closed, she leaned into the breeze rolling off the water and gave it a good, long sniff.

'Me haere tātou,' she said.

Māmā could smell the wind and know whether it was a good day for fishing. She was always right, which meant we never had to waste a day. I didn't know anyone else like her. I wished I could be special like her.

We pushed our wooden dinghy out onto the water and rowed out until Māmā said to stop. She carefully lined the boat up with the shore and the cardinal directions to find our fishing place. We had to stick to our spot. Māmā said a karakia to Tangaroa, and then she spat on the bait. 'Te māunu, te māunu,' she said to the fish. 'Tīkina mai.' We cast the hooks into the sea.

Pāpā had a strong nose and was good with a gun. He'd brought back a pig that morning. After he'd dealt with it, he gave me a package, with a glint in his eye.

'From Santa,' he said. It was already January. 'Santa got lost. He had to drop it off by aeroplane.' I tore open the brown paper. Bright blue mittens with stars on them. Although it was summer, I put them on and wore them until Māmā ordered me to scrape the fur off the pig. Santa had flown an aeroplane to the Hokianga just for me.

* * *

On my twelfth birthday, Māmā sat me down in front of the house and chopped off my long hair with rusty dressmaking scissors. I felt like I was being punished, but I didn't know why. That night, I had the same dream as I'd had the night before, and the night before that. It began with me sound asleep in my bed. When you dream you are doing what you are actually doing, it feels like real life. It's the scariest thing ever. In the dream, I wake up to a sense of dread crushing me like a stone slab, in the deepest, darkest of nights. A night so intense it can be felt. A night where nothing can be seen. I will myself to get up and turn on the light. I inch barefoot across the cold dirt floor. I have trouble walking again, like when I was little. When I finally make it to the wall, I flick the switch, but nothing happens. The night still envelops me. I want to cry out but I am struck dumb. I want to flee but I am nailed to the spot. No matter how many times I try to turn on the light, I am alone in the darkness.

* * *

I loved English; especially poetry. It reminded me of the way the kaumātua speak on the paepae. My teacher, Miss Kingi, took an interest in my poems and loaned me books from her personal library. We didn't have any books at home.

'You'll go pōrangi if you keep looking at those Pākehā books!' Māmā said.

She truly believed that, and feared for me, so I would read in an old pūriri tree, perched in its branches where she couldn't see me.

Māmā thought I was still out with Pāpā cutting tea tree. After he and I had cut a big stack for the fire, Pāpā whistled for the dogs and headed into the bush with his gun. That was my chance to retrieve a book I'd hidden in the woodshed.

I liked it up there in the tree. I imagined it was my house. Each limb was a different room. I sat on the widest branch, which was my parlour. It had a plush red couch and a record player in the corner. There were pictures on the walls of classical Greek ruins in gilt frames. My doll Kuini was wedged into the branches.

I opened up the worn blue volume of Shakespeare's plays with my teacher's handwriting scrawled in the margins, and read a couple of lines for Kuini:

Full fathom five thy father lies;
Of his bones are coral made;
Those are pearls that were his eyes;
Nothing of him that doth fade,
But doth suffer a sea-change
Into something rich and strange.

'The photographer from the *Northern Age* is here,' said Miss Kingi, smiling. I smoothed my hair down. I had washed it last night, starched my school blouse and mended the loose binding on my blazer.

'So, is this the poet? Lovely! Hello, dear. Now, stand over here by the door, that's a good girl,' said a Pākehā man with a bulky camera around his neck. I stood there looking at the ground while the other kids gawked and pointed.

'Miss! Why is Nerissa getting her picture taken? What about us?'

'Her poems have been published. If you apply yourself to your studies, Hohepa, maybe you'll get your photograph in the paper next.'

I wished everyone would stop talking and go away.

'Now don't be shy, dear. Show us that lovely face of yours,' said the photographer.

I lifted my chin and looked into the camera.

I ran down to the letterbox after breakfast. Pāpā read the newspaper to study English. Sometimes he'd invite Pākehā over for a cuppa so he could practise. I snatched the paper up and ran all the way to my tree and climbed up into its reaches. There it was. My picture in grainy black and white, and my poem, with my name underneath. I read the opening lines aloud to Kuini:

Spade
Dig your sharpened edge into the flesh of the soil
let it turn over the soft turf and
fling it high upon mounting mud.
Let water find its way through
the disturbed earth …

Pāpā and I had been fixing fences at the far end of the farm. We rode back on our horses in our usual silence. I wondered how I could steal away to read a book of poems by Hone Tūwhare, but when we got back Pāpā sent me straight inside.

'Māmā wants you,' he said.

I tilted my head. There was something in his tone.

Māmā was standing by the wood stove with something in her hand. She fixed me with a hard look, and made sure I was watching as she opened the black mouth of the stove. I knew what she was holding. I'd had several poems published by now, in several issues of the *Northern Age* and even a couple of magazines. She fed the fire with my only copies. The flames burned brighter for a few seconds as the words on the page dissolved into ashes.

* * *

I sat on the back of the milk truck with all my possessions in a satchel beside me. I'd left Kuini in the tree. I couldn't take her with me to St Anne's Hostel for Māori Girls. The others might laugh. Pāpā stood at the gate alone, straight-backed and forlorn. I watched him recede into the distance through clouds of dust.

Little Miss Paranoid

Half a watermelon, the pink scooped out, edge cut into a zigzag, filled with fruit salad. After it's all gone, Uncle Shane who isn't really my uncle, squashes the watermelon onto Dad's head and the juice drips down his face. The grown-ups are drinking rum and Cokes. Dad picks Mum up and throws her into Uncle Shane's pool. Once I fell in and sank to the bottom in slow motion. It was pretty relaxing, but then Aunty Diane pulled me out by the hair. She's not really my aunty either. In the car on the way home Mum says to Dad that Aunty Diane used to be a stripper, which means a rude lady who takes all her clothes off.

Sister Mary told me to read a book to the class because I'm the cleverest. She turned to page three and said if you don't know this word, just say *rainbow fish*, which is dumb because I already know it says *jellyfish*.

'Okay, children. Write a story – *What I did in the school holidays*.'

Me and my little brother and Mum and Dad visited Nana Merau. It took ages to get there. We had to go over the bridge and on the motorway way past Tip Top Corner. Nana Merau's house has long pink curtains that are always closed and she has the lights on so it seems like night-time. She is short and brown with long black hair like Mum. She gave me a brooch with a silhouette of a princess on it. It's called a cameo. I already knew that.

I start writing with my new fountain pen. It's blue ink and you can't press down too hard.

'How do you spell "Merau"?' I ask Sister Mary.

'Beg your pardon, dear?'

'Merau.'

'M, E, A, D, O, W.'

I know Nana's name isn't Meadow, but I write it down anyway.

I have a glow-in-the-dark crucifix and a picture of Jesus with the sacred heart on my bedroom wall. The cross is from the Catholic shop in town. I always look at it at night but it never glows like it's supposed to. I pray to Jesus every night too, but he never says anything back. At school in Christian Living, Sister Zita says we must have faith. It must be my fault Jesus doesn't reply. I ask him to make my parents happy so they will stop fighting, and to give them more money. Everyone else has flash cars like Rovers, not a stink one like ours. The only other Māori in my class got dropped off in an old bomb too, and I heard Katrina Beets say 'Is that Jerome's car?' and she looked really disgusted. I went to her birthday and her house was really flash. They had food like olives and parmesan cheese, and a trampoline, a pool and two cars. One of them is a Jag. My dad is a Pākehā but he isn't rich. Mum is a Māori and is definitely not rich at all.

Te Unga Waka is the Māori church, and I hate going there because the service is all in Māori and I can't understand it so it's even more boring than the service at St Mary's. At least there I get to work the overhead projector because I'm clever and I always remember the song lyrics have to go on backwards. I also hate it because Dad won't drive us there, so Mum and my little brother and me have to take three buses. It takes ages. We put on our church clothes and walk with Mum to the bus stop.

'What's your name?' the bus driver says to Mum.

He has hairy hands and stares at Mum in the rearview mirror. My little brother kicks the seat and I think about biting him. We change buses and finally we arrive at Te Unga Waka. I hate church, but the carvings inside are alright. I like the one in the middle sticking its tongue out. Also it's okay when Mum sings her action songs with Rangimārie and does poi. She's the shortest and the prettiest. My favourite one is when they go takiri takiri takiri hi auē takiri takiri takiri hi auē hi. But the speeches go on and on for ages, and I'm always starving. Sometimes I go and sit in the tree outside and pretend it's my house and look down at the people below and call them fucken little bastards, quietly so they can't hear me.

My mum calls me Little Miss Paranoid. I don't know what that means but I know it isn't good.

Here is a photo of me when I was a baby at the beach. I'm sitting on a really big towel because Mum said if the tiniest bit of sand got on me I would scream my head off.

My father has something hidden in his wardrobe.

'Do you think your mother will like this?' he says, and shows me a flowing dressing gown with lilies and roses on it. I hold the silky fabric against my cheek.

'Yes,' I say. 'She'll love it.'

On Christmas Day Mum unwraps her present from my father and says, 'It's too long.' She makes breakfast in it with a sour face and never wears it again. I secretly try it on and imagine being a grown-up lady who hates nice things. I turn this way, and then that. I frown at myself in the mirror.

And then one day my father is gone, and there's another man at our table having tea. We leave our street with the nice park across the road and move to Ōtara. Tin City, it's called, because the shops have metal roller doors to protect them. On my first day at my new school, a girl in my class throws a desk through the window and the teacher cries because someone stole twenty bucks from her handbag. We do spelling and the other kids are way behind me and I get bored. On the weekend we go to the flea market at the town centre. Outside a shoe shop, two big fat ladies are having a fight. They knock the stands over and throw shoes at each other like ninja stars.

I hate it here.

Uncle Tommy drove off the skyline and my other uncles found him in his car, so we drive up north for the tangi. It's a really long way, and the road is full of potholes. I lean my forehead against the window and watch those things that look like matchsticks on the side of the road flash past. The skyline is windy and narrow and steep. Aunty says to Mum they reckon Uncle was drunk. Just before we get to the marae, Aunty stops the car and her and Mum get some kawakawa from the side of the road and we put it on our heads like crowns. We get to the marae and the old ladies call us on and Mum starts to tangitangi. I've never heard her sound like that before and it's the saddest sound in the whole world. Then we have to take our shoes off to go into the wharenui, and I worry that my best shiny black shoes, the ones with the little ankle strap that are for church, will get mixed up and lost or, worst of all, paru. I hate my shoes getting paru. Then we go in and Mum cries so much when she sees Uncle in his coffin, and she needs a hanky for all the hūpē. Then we have to kiss him and he's so cold, like a stone. Then we sit down on the mattresses and there are karakia and speeches, which are boring because they're all in Māori, and singing, which is okay because I know some of the words. Mum pokes me in the back to get up and sing with her. Then it's time for a kai, and we go outside and my shoes are missing. I tiptoe around in my tights because I don't want them to get all paru, and shuffle shoes around. Then I see a girl with a snotty nose in a stripy turtleneck stomping around in my best shoes, her bare feet shoved inside them, outside in the mud. I cry and Mum says she's your cousin stop being a tangiweto and gets them back, but now I don't like them any more. Then it's boil-up for tea. Yuck. I like the fried bread though. Then it's time for a shower because Mum says it will be too busy in the morning. The concrete floor is really cold and the hot water runs out while there's still shampoo in my hair. Then me and my cousins play on the mattresses in the wharenui while the grown-ups have a cup of tea in the wharekai and we jump around and have a pillow fight. An old lady tells us off. She has whiskers and is really mean and looks like a witch. Uncle Tommy doesn't mind us playing; he's dead. I wonder what it's like being dead. Is he in heaven looking down and seeing what we're all doing? At St Mary's they say if you're not good you'll go to hell, and I don't know if he was good because he was in the Stormtroopers.

The next day I try to read my book, but Aunty sees me reading in the wharenui and says, 'Maia needs a mate,' and makes my cousins play with me. I really want to read my book and I don't want anyone to play with. I make my cousins play schools and I'm the teacher and I make them all read and do homework. They say playing schools is boring; let's go catch frogs in the creek and squirt water out their bums at each other. I hate the sound of that, so I read the *Northern Advocate* in the wharekai and my aunties and uncles laugh at me and call me kuia. I don't see what's so funny about reading the newspaper.

The next day is the burial, and a big fat Stormtrooper helps carry the coffin with Uncle in it, and he's wearing a patch that says Ōtara Stormtroopers and it has a skull on it and a swastika. He's not wearing any shoes. After, we throw dirt on Uncle's coffin in the ground, and then we wash our hands at the tap outside the urupā and Mum flicks her hands to take the tapu off and I copy her. Then it's the hākari and all the best kai is put out: chop suey, raw fish, mussels, hāngī and steam pudding. At the kids' table there's fizzy drinks and jelly and ice cream. My cousins keep asking me why I look like a honky. It's weird being white at the marae. I don't look like I belong here. But I do.

Paradise

Maia hadn't slept on the overnight flight. Dazed, she floated down a moving walkway through the calm of Narita Airport. Then it was all clamour and rush to catch trains into Tokyo. At the turnstile she grabbed a Japanese girl's subway ticket by mistake, and the girl cried out in dismay.

Maia struggled to keep up with Laura, who strode through the sea of Japanese. The humidity made her wilt in her winter dress. She'd never felt air this thick before: heavy and laced with diesel and soy sauce. From the back of a cab, the seats covered in a spotless doily-like lace, Maia marvelled at the crowds, the giant TV screens playing frenetic ads at high volume, the colourful billboards, the incomprehensible kanji characters. Even the trees around the Imperial Palace looked Japanese. As they clambered out, the taxi driver made protesting sounds as Maia tried to close the door.

'Don't do that; you'll break it! It closes automatically,' said Laura.

The sign on the drab block of apartments said 'Akasaka Weekly Mansion'.

'When a Japanese tells you they live in a mansion, this is what they mean,' said Laura.

Their room was two single beds, with side tables. Laura eased herself out onto the balcony and lit a cigarette.

'I'm shattered,' Maia said, and collapsed onto her bed. Laura had already claimed the best one near the window.

'It's Friday night! We gotta work.'

The two women jostled for position in front of the only mirror, curled their hair, carefully applied heavy make-up and shoved some dresses into a bag.

Maia and Laura made their way through crowded plazas to an entrance with a brass plaque that said: 'SHINJUKU PARADISE – GENTLEMEN'S CLUB'. Stairs led them underground to a stage with a pole on it. There were booths and tables with red velvet club chairs clustered around the stage. The walls were mirrored, and a disco ball cast a spell over the empty room. The bartender was cutting limes, and greeted them with a cheery 'Ohayō!' Maia recognised one of the four Japanese words she knew.

'Why did he say good morning?'

'This *is* our morning. You're a vampire now.'

They went to the dressing room and joined fifteen other girls. Two of them were arguing in Hebrew and wore G-strings. They stopped abruptly when they saw Maia and whispered to each other. In the back corner, three blonde Australians discussed boob jobs.

Maia put on a black, sheer dress and the lucite heels that Laura had instructed her to buy. Laura called them 'stripper heels', and Maia saw that all the girls were wearing the clear shoes, except for a Japanese girl in sandals. Maia was glad she had the right shoes. She checked herself out in the mirror. Long, dead straight, jet-black hair, a nice face, big tits and a slim body.

'This is Eden; she's from New Zealand too,' Laura said to Joy, a girl with dirty blonde hair and a tattoo of the Grim Reaper on her back. Joy glanced at Maia with sad, blue eyes and said nothing. She took a sip from a foil pouch.

'What's that?' asked Maia.

'An energy jelly drink. I didn't eat today. Kinda weird, but you get used to it.'

'Smells like rank pussy in here,' Laura said.

Maia stood by the bar doing shots with Laura and studied the girls onstage. They danced mainly to R&B and hiphop. She watched as dancers crawled up to the men sitting around the stage and drew money out from their wallets with sultry long looks. One of the Australians, Cherry, climbed up the pole, flipped herself upside down, clung on to it with her legs and slithered off her top. Her implants looked ready to burst through her skin.

'I can't do this,' Maia said.

She thought back to that coffee she'd had in Wellington with Laura, who had just returned from her first stint in Japan with Gucci this and Prada that. Maia, an underpaid and overworked single mother, begged her for help. She hadn't thought this through.

'Ha; don't worry. Pole tricks aren't important. Keep it sexy; you'll be fine,' said Laura.

'And now, we have next on stage … the lovely Miss … Eden!' the DJ announced.

'Eden needs another shot,' Laura said to the bartender.

Maia looked out into the darkness. Men gazed up at her like she was the sun. She grabbed hold of the pole and spun around it clumsily. She pouted and leaned over; she let herself slide down the wall in what she hoped was a seductive way. Every time she caught a glimpse of herself in the myriad reflective surfaces, she felt ridiculous; caught in prisms of mortification. When a heavily tattooed gaijin customer beckoned her over with a note in his hand, it was a relief. It gave her something to do. She slunk over and let him put it in her cleavage. Laura gave her a thumbs-up from the bar. When her song finally ended, Maia gathered up her dress, pulled it over her head and raced off the stage.

'You have a request, Miss Eden,' said Little Joe, the Nigerian floor manager, steering Maia to a table.

Customers from Saudi Arabia.

'I asked for a girl from New Zealand,' said one of the men. 'Such a beautiful place. Maybe that is why you are so beautiful.'

'Oh, you've been?'

'Yes, I loved it. Wonderful. But in my country, we don't like other men to look at our women.'

A couple of drinks in, she noticed him glancing over at the booths at the back of the club, where customers were getting lap dances. She took him by the hand and led him to a row of plush round chairs. She leaned over him and pushed her breasts in his face, while looking over at what the other girls were doing. Lots of slow grinding in the shadows. He put his hands on her waist and looked up at her. A blacklight made his teeth and the whites of his eyes glow.

After six songs, she asked for her money. His face darkened.

'A girl like you isn't worth even 5 yen,' he spat.

The Nigerian dance manager came over.

'Everything okay, Eden?' he said.

The Arab paid.

After work finished at three, Maia and Laura met some of the other dancers at Half Time, an American-style bar with dark wooden decor and vintage signs.

'So, what do you all do back home?' said Nina, a redhead from New York.

'I was a sergeant in the Israeli army,' said Noa. She had large dark eyes and thick black hair. Her friend Alana was tall and lanky with frizzy hair. They were often in trouble at the club for arguing with the customers, managers and each other.

'Wow. How was that?' said Maia.

'What do you think? It fucking sucked!'

'She was my boss,' said Alana. 'I was just a private.'

'When we first saw you walk into the dressing room tonight, we said, "That girl doesn't belong here,"' Noa said.

'Why?' said Maia.

'Too beautiful,' said Alana.

Maia and Laura wove through the narrow aisles of Don Quijote, a twenty-four-hour discount store full of snacks, souvenirs, make-up, appliances and sex toys. Laura pointed out some squeezable stress balls shaped like tits in the children's toy section.

'This country is twisted,' said Maia.

'Ah, here's the costume section,' Laura said. She combed through stacks of costume packs. Slutty nurse, slutty witch, slutty air hostess. Maia wanted something Japanese-y. Slutty pilot, slutty fortune teller, slutty policewoman.

'Oh look,' said Maia, and held up a pack that displayed a picture of a Japanese woman posing coyly in a blouse with a navy-blue sailor-style collar, red ribbon and pleated skirt. 'Think I could pull this off?'

'That's a Japanese schoolgirl uniform,' said Laura.

'Perfect.'

All the girls were in costume for Halloween. There was a genie, several French maids, Alice in Wonderland, a honeybee, a dominatrix, Cleopatra … The genie winked and clasped her hands together as Maia came out of the dressing room in her schoolgirl uniform.

'Your wish is my command,' the genie said.

The club was decorated with fake spiderwebs. A waiter dressed as Superman brought her a double vodka cranberry to drink while she waited to be sat with customers. Her new customer, Kyomin, rumoured to be Korean mafia, came in while she was on stage. He was in his early thirties, tall and well dressed. He had an attractive face, with wide, high cheekbones. Kyomin strolled up to the stage, holding bills out in front of him like a fan, and spun her around slowly as he stuffed ichiman yen notes all around her G-string, making a skirt of money. Everyone in the club clapped. The other girls looked jealous as Maia strutted around with a thousand dollars in her underwear. Back at the table, Kyomin presented her with a Prada bag, which drew even more envy.

'But it's not even my birthday! You are so yasashii, ne.' She gave him a peck on the cheek, and sat next to him most of the night. As soon as a cigarette touched his lips, she had a lighter ready. She sat up straight, kept his glass full, amused his friends. Kyomin stroked her arm lightly.

'Your skin, so smooth. Korean women have very smooth skin. Like snake,' he said.

He left after leaving her a generous tip, and promised to visit her again soon.

'Eden, you have a request,' the floor manager said, motioning to a middle-aged Japanese salaryman sitting alone. Maia had already made plenty of money and felt like riding out the rest of the night flirting with the Japanese bartender with the spiky hair. She went over grudgingly. The man was drinking mizuwari, whiskey and water, the salaryman's drink of choice. She hated the smell of it.

'Sekushī,' said the man, admiring her school uniform. His eyes lingered over her legs. She had on the long baggy socks that all the schoolgirls wore. He had a comb-over. Maia didn't feel like talking, so she dragged him off to private dance. When they came back to the table, his eyes were moist.

'Your costume very good. Looks like my daughter.'

※ ※ ※

Maia was on her seventh double vodka and cranberry of the night. Her last customer said, 'I'll give you 50,000 yen if you come back to my hotel.' He was owlish, in metal-framed glasses.

Maia heard herself say, 'Sure'.

He waited at a discreet distance outside the club. Maia followed him through Kabukichō to a nearby hotel. She helped herself to a drink from the minibar. He took his shirt off, revealing a faint pink rash all over his back and torso, and sat on the bed. He motioned for her to join him. She remained standing, gulped down her drink and poured another one.

'If you don't pay me 100,000 yen, I'll go downstairs and tell the staff at the front desk that you tried to rape me,' she said.

His eyes widened. 'I'm a professional; a nice guy. Please. I don't want any trouble.'

Maia struck him across the face, making him cry out.

'I don't have that much cash on me.'

'We'll go to an ATM.'

'No, please,' he said.

'Get! Up! Get! My! Fucking! Money!' Maia punctuated each word with swift punches and kicks. She kicked over his suitcase, and threw his shirt at him.

'Put your fucking clothes back on.'

She frog-marched him out of the room and into the elevator. As they passed the hotel staff in the lobby, she poked him in the ribs and flashed him a warning look. Once outside, she pushed him along the street, her fist in the small of his back, to a nearby ATM. He looked absolutely wretched. Maia wanted to laugh. *He's acting like I have a gun pointed at him.* He handed her 100,000 yen. She prodded him in the back.

'Gimme 50,000 more.'

It was daylight. Crows were feasting on trash outside the apartment building. Maia's hangover was starting to kick in, and she didn't have her sunglasses. She bumped into Laura at the entrance; she was just arriving home herself, looking wired.

'Where have *you* been?' demanded Laura.

'I could ask you the same question.'

Laura said that she and some other dancers had been hired by yakuza to dress up in cosplay costumes and dance at a party. Afterwards she had freebased cocaine with a contraption that the yakuza boss had pulled out of his briefcase.

Maia filled her in on her night.

'You're a crazy bitch,' said Laura.

'What did he think I was, a whore?' said Maia.

Maia woke up late the next afternoon. She raised her head and saw the pile of 150,000 yen next to her bed.

Laura was sitting up in bed, hair wrapped up in a towel, staring at a Hello Kitty mirror with tweezers in her hand. She looked over at Maia and arched a freshly plucked eyebrow.

'How's the head?'

'Not great.'

'You can't pull stunts like that. You'll get thrown in jail.'

'Yeah, I know.'

'We have to suffer for this money.'

'I thought we were gonna be artists. What are we doing here?'

'Our lives are art,' said Laura. 'Now get up, we're going to watch sumo wrestling with my customer in Ginza. We have front row seats.'

Autumn Feeling

The maples are red and yellow. The light makes Akiko wistful, though the earth turning away from the sun is a relief. Summer had been especially humid this year. She hadn't left the house much; had spent long afternoons laid out under the aircon with her Yorkshire terrier Tracey, an ice-cold oshibori pressed to her temples.

She hails a taxi to Tsukiji Fish Market, and heads to her favourite stall.

'Your best sanma, please,' says Akiko. 'I'm meeting my son's wife from New Zealand today.'

'Nyū Jīrando desu ka,' says the fishmonger. 'Surely a nice place, but so far away.'

He selects a fish and offers it to her for inspection. It's so fresh and firm it stands upright in his fist like a sword. She asks for five, and wrings her hands while he wraps them. Her new daughter-in-law doesn't speak Japanese. How are they supposed to communicate? Can she use chopsticks? Will she know to use the toilet slippers?

She'd always wanted a daughter, but had two sons. Her eldest, Ryō, married a woman from Osaka. Yayoi's accent and casual manner grated. As for her dress sense, well. Let's not even think about the time Yayoi wore ripped jeans to Hibiki's piano recital. But at least she is Japanese.

Dai had dropped another bombshell yesterday. Not only is his new wife a gaijin; she has a daughter.

The familiar purr of the Mercedes outside prompts Akiko to call out to her husband Koji, 'They're here.' She takes off her apron to greet her son and his new family at the front door.

She scrutinises them as they get out of the car. A burgeoning pot belly is visible through Dai's shirt. What has this new wife been feeding him? She is slim and attractive, but her top is a little low cut, and she looks far too young to be the mother of an eight-year-old. The child is cute, with her long brown hair in a ponytail, and she has brown skin, unlike her mother. They look more like sisters than mother and daughter. Aria could pass as Japanese, but for her large eyes.

Autumn Feeling

Akiko and Koji bow slightly.

'Hajimemashite,' Maia says, and bows awkwardly, before handing Akiko an airport shopping bag. 'Tsumaranai mono desuga. It's nothing much.'

'Nanimo sonna ki wo tsukawanakute ii noni. Arigatō ne,' Akiko says. 'Please come in.'

They follow Akiko upstairs to the living room. She reaches into the bag and pulls out a T-shirt with the Sydney Olympics logo on it, and leans back in her new massage chair and lays it over her chest.

'Owari dayo,' Akiko says.

Maia looks to Dai for a translation.

'She loves it.'

They sit at the kitchen table, and Akiko serves lunch on her best plates from Kyoto. Crisp, whole sanma salted then grilled to perfection, with a mizuna salad, miso soup and the pickles that Dai likes best.

'Itadakimasu,' everyone says, including Maia and Aria. They know the basics at least.

Akiko eyes the pair as they eat their rice. They leave their bowls on the table, and bring the rice to their lips in an ungainly manner.

'Table manners say a lot about upbringing,' says Akiko.

'Shōganai,' says Dai. 'They aren't Japanese. Remember when you and Dad slurped on pasta in Italy like it was ramen? It was so embarrassing.'

'How are you supposed to eat it?' says Koji.

'Not like that,' says Dai. 'When in Rome, deshō.'

'Ā, sō.'

'What's the weather like in New Zealand now?' Akiko says.

Dai translates Maia's response. 'It's spring now. A little cold still.'

'Oh? New Zealand has four seasons like Japan then?' Akiko says.

Dai translates for Maia, who looks confused and murmurs something.

'She says many countries have four seasons.'

'Oh, but Japan is quite special in that respect,' says Akiko. 'Tell her we eat sanma in autumn. Aki yo ne. Autumn feeling.'

They all fall silent and concentrate on eating. Maia struggles with the bones and Dai shows her how to lift the spine out.

Maia says something to Dai and he laughs.

'What?' Akiko says.

'She asked why Japanese people always talk about food.'

'Safe topic dayo,' says Koji.

'She also asked why there are no pictures of me and Ryō,' says Dai.

Akiko hadn't noticed. There were framed pictures of Akiko's beloved Yorkshire terrier everywhere. Tracey at the dog park, Tracey in her stroller, Tracey at a café.

'If you give a dog love, they give it back,' Akiko says.

She had given her sons the best of everything. During the Bubble era she took them to breakfast at the New Otani every morning, or whichever upscale hotel took her fancy. Those days were the best. Everyone thought they'd be rich forever. She sent the boys to the top kindergarten, schools and university in Tokyo. They did homestays in the US to learn to speak English fluently. Akiko was president of the PTA. She had done everything right as a mother. Now both her sons live in the block of apartments she and Koji own, rent free, as neither have proper jobs. Since leaving his high-flying advertising exec position, Ryō had set up an internet café that had failed, and was now practically a shut-in, and Dai had become a DJ. Playing records in nightclubs was hardly something Akiko could take seriously. It certainly did not give her any bragging rights when she met her friends in Ginza for lunch. Where had she gone wrong?

On TV, a Yorkshire terrier with tartan bows in its perfectly groomed fur gambols through a plume of bubbles.

'Look – it's Tracey!' says Koji.

'Sugoi!' says Dai.

Tracey trots into the room.

'Wow, kawaii,' says Aria, and gets up to pat the dog. Akiko smiles.

'Tracey got paid goman yen for that commercial,' says Akiko. 'Even she has a job, and she's just a dog.'

Dai bows his head.

'Sorry,' he says.

'If sorry was good enough, we wouldn't need police,' says Akiko.

'The fish is delicious,' Maia says.

* * *

They don't know what it's like. To never know your mother. To be raised by others; people who could never give you a mother's love. Your true origins never spoken about. Akiko had done her best. When she'd come home from cram school aged twelve and found her brother hanging, she'd cleaned up the mess. What else was there to do?

* * *

After Ladurée macarons and tea for dessert, Akiko presents Maia with a large Louis Vuitton tote bag.

'She used to put Tracey in that when she was a puppy,' says Dai.

'That's right,' says Koji.

Maia's cheeks turn pink. She stands up and bows deeply to Akiko, then sits back down next to Dai on the sofa.

'Shiawase,' Maia says.

It has been a very long time since Akiko has heard someone say that. When was the last time she'd been truly, deeply happy?

'Honto ni? Really?'

'Honto shiawase.'

Akiko thaws a little, but how can this young gaijin with a child, still a child herself, manage here in Japan? How did she even end up in Tokyo? Is she working in Roppongi?

'Taihen,' she says, softly. Maia doesn't understand, of course. Dai looks at the floor.

'Taihen nano yo,' she repeats, not unkindly. The struggle will be real.

Spirit House

It had been two years since the great tsunami, and there was no sign of Phi Phi Charlie, the budget resort that I thought of as Shangri-la. The cabins under the coconut trees were gone. Every ramshackle structure on that stretch of sandy white beachfront had been erased: the beach bar built around a gnarled banyan tree, those wooden bungalows you could barely see for vegetation. Now there was only rubble and empty space. To make matters worse, construction of a sprawling concrete hotel was in full swing. On that first visit to Phi Phi Island a few years before, my only worry had been a coconut falling from those Dr Seuss trees and hitting me on the head.

'Let's face it,' I'd said to the handsome Israeli I'd lured back to my cabin. 'Death by coconut would be embarrassing.'

'You wouldn't care, because you'd be dead.'

'Oh, I'd care.'

The wooden longtails moored at the edge of Loh Dalum had prows that jutted up like Māori waka, adorned with pink and yellow garlands instead of carving. Aria and I walked down the beach in new bikinis and matching Barbie-pink mani/pedis, looking for a guide to take us snorkelling and island hopping. Someone good-looking and friendly, with a nice boat and free fins.

I spotted a guide I recognised. Kasem was nimbly leaping around his longtail with coils of rope, wearing a faded Nirvana 'Come as you are' T-shirt and jeans cut off at the knee to reveal thick, muscular calves. He had taken me snorkelling on my first trip to Phi Phi, and I'd hired him every day for the duration of my holiday. I remembered how he'd expertly cut up a pineapple and thrown chunks of it into the sea around me, and laughed as I shrieked while the tropical fish nibbled at my limbs. All those little mouths had creeped me out.

'You're alive,' I said, greeting him warmly like an old friend.

'Lucky, yes very lucky,' Kasem said, smiling but not quite meeting my eye. He didn't remember me. I felt stupid for thinking he would. How could he distinguish me from the hordes of tourists that descend on this place? A life highlight for me was just another day's work for him. We agreed on a price for him to take us to Maya Bay.

The overcast day made the colours appear even more saturated. The water was a vibrant shade of emerald. Aria and I chatted and laughed as the longtail skimmed and bounced over the waves, but we fell silent as we drew near the limestone cliffs of Phi Phi Lei. I remembered the first time I saw those massive vertical faces of stone rise up from the ocean. Beauty always has an edge that hurts. When I looked upon those cliffs, I heard the voice of God.

'Well, what did God say?' the handsome Israeli said, in bed. He had bright blue eyes fringed with long lashes. I thought about not answering because I didn't want to sound corny, but even today it still chokes me up to think about all that heavy, heavy beauty.

'Listen.'

'What?'

'He said, "Listen."'

Kasem cut the motor of the longtail and threw the anchor over.

'Good place to snorkel,' he said, and gave us a thumbs-up. 'You find Nemo.'

We perched on the edge of the boat.

'What if there are still bodies down there?' said Aria, eyeing the emerald waters.

'The sea is much clearer than it was when I was here last,' I replied. Maybe the tsunami had been a giant clearing away. Mother Nature strikes back kind of thing. Aria's large, dark eyes still fretted. I took her hand and together we leaped feet first into the Andaman Sea.

We floated above a garden of giant brain coral and undulating anemones and kept our legs up to avoid the long spikes of sea urchins. Tiny silver fish glittered and shone like tinsel twisting in the light. A cloud of angel fish surrounded us and drew us into their hive mind. We swam as one with the school, darting this way then that, and glided above and around rocks and giant clams at exhilarating speed, before they ejected us back into singular human consciousness. We clambered back on the boat, elated. Aria couldn't stop talking.

'That was so fun! I love snorkelling! Can we go every day?'

The fins that had made us so quick and agile in the water now made us step awkwardly. We clowned around a bit before kicking them off. Kasem cut up a watermelon and we crammed it into our mouths, grinning at each other as we ate. Aria sat on her blue striped beach towel and leaned back to dry off in the sun.

Kasem guided the boat to a sliver of beach teeming with monkeys. A bold one with silvery hair leaped up on the bow and held a tiny wrinkled palm out for fruit. Kasem took a picture of us with the disposable underwater camera I'd bought at the airport. In the picture Aria and I smile broadly, with tanned faces dewy from the humidity.

Maya Bay itself was a let-down. There were too many boats; far more than before. A lone red flip flop washed up in the surf. The beach was covered in trash.

'Who would litter in a place like this?' Aria said.

We were part of the problem by being there. Two men wearing gold jewellery waved and greeted us. I scowled back.

We woke to a brooding kind of day, dark clouds gathering and a heaviness in the air. Aria leafed through a magazine while I read a battered paperback. Every now and then, we'd tire of reading and ask each other random questions.

'Do you wanna know what my favourite word is?' Aria asked, shielding her face from the sun with her hand.

'What is it?' I asked.

'Garden,' Aria said. 'I like the way it sounds. Do you know what my favourite food is?'

'Pizza.'

'No. It's shōgayaki,' she said. 'You should know that.'

She was right. I should.

'Do you have a boyfriend?' I asked.

'No,' she said. 'Do you?'

'Yeah, you met him. That French guy.'

Aria frowned.

'Why do you keep going for DJs? They're losers.'

I remembered when I'd introduced Aria to my new boyfriend. When out of his earshot, she'd asked if he was rich, and I'd shaken my head.

'Isn't he gonna buy me a pony?' Aria had said and stamped her foot in her best impression of a spoiled brat.

'I bumped into Dai the other day in Daikanyama,' Aria said. 'It was weird. Like seeing a ghost or something.'

'Yeah, he mentioned he'd seen you.'

I remembered the last time I'd spoken to my ex-husband on the phone. He'd complained that I was too lenient on Aria; that I let her do whatever she wanted.

'She's too free,' he'd said. 'Like a bird or something.'

After lunch Aria and I lolled around the lagoon, the water nearly the same temperature as the air. The dark clouds that had been hanging over us all day finally burst and pelted us with warm tropical rain. We splashed each other. She showed me how she could make a wave ripple up and down her abs. My attempts to imitate her made her howl with laughter. Flopping around in the warm lagoon while it rained was like being a child playing in the bath with the shower running. Finally, we lay on our backs, submerged like crocodiles with only our eyes above the surface. Phi Phi Lei in the distance looked skeletal, a circle of giant knucklebones in the middle of the ocean.

'I wish I had my camera,' I said.

'Just remember it,' Aria said.

Back in our room, we threw on new beachy clothes that we'd haggled over in the market: a cropped aquamarine T-shirt and denim mini for me, a cobalt blue sarong with silvery threads shot through it and tank top for Aria.

'Are you wearing that?' she said, eyeing my skirt. 'Don't you think it's a bit hoe-ish?'

'Where did you learn that word?'

'It would look better on me,' she said. 'You're a bit fat.'

We walked down the bustling village street, looking for a place to have dinner.

We peered into one place that was playing seventies' music. Aria laughed.

'That sounds like porn music,' she said.

'How do you know what porn music sounds like?'

We kept walking, past shops selling triangular Thai pillows, hippy jewellery and racks of colourful fishermen's pants.

'I wish Nana was here,' said Aria.

I didn't say anything. She'd visited us in Tokyo the previous winter, and I'd found it difficult.

'Don't be angry at Nana,' Aria said. 'She's getting old.'

We stopped by a shop that sold soap carved into intricate flowers.

'Get her something,' I said, and handed her some money. 'Send her a postcard.'

Aria was fascinated by the spirit houses, the shrines outside every building and shop, built to shelter the spirits of the land. Roofed structures perched atop pillars, with ladders leading down to the earth. They were colourful and laden with offerings. Even the 7-Eleven had one.

'Look at the people,' she said, pointing at figurines of an old man and woman sitting inside a white and gold spirit house outside one of the larger restaurants. 'Who are they supposed to be?'

'Ancestors, I'd say.'

'Take a picture of me,' she said, and posed next to the spirit house with a peace sign, Japanese style. When I developed the film later, Aria is surrounded by glowing orbs.

Aria and I took a table directly on the sand.

'Tonight, we shall eat like queens,' I declared, and ordered a couple of lobsters.

We were watching a peddler throw a toy with flashing lights into the night sky when a couple of men stopped by our table. Olive-skinned with black hair, they looked to be in their thirties.

'Would you like a drink?' the taller one asked Aria.

Aria's cheeks went pink. She looked at me.

'What do you think you're doing?' I said to him.

'I'm offering your friend a drink.'

'She's my daughter.'

'You're Mama?' he said. He looked at me and shook his head. 'Wow ... we saw you two on the beach today. We thought you were friends.'

'She's fourteen.'

As they slunk off, Aria smirked at me.

'Can I have a beer, Mum?'

'You're underage.'

'Please. It's our last night!'

'Okay. Just this once. Can't believe they thought I was the grumpy older friend.'

The waiter brought over two bottles of Singha beer.

'To life,' I said.

'I'll drink to that,' Aria said.

* * *

There are two kinds of people: people who stay and people who leave.

I don't judge people who stay. It just wasn't for me. I have a vivid memory of being ten years old and gazing at the green hills that surrounded our village and feeling like I couldn't breathe. I had some kind of profound yearning; a lump in the throat that was almost painful. I wanted to get out, get away from those green hills penning me in and see something – anything – different. If the world is a book, why would I only read the first page?

Idol

I try to sleep but the cockroaches are so bad I have to wear earplugs so they don't crawl inside my ears. It happened last summer. So gross, MAJI DE KIMOKATTA. (╬ ಠ益ಠ) It was still wriggling when the doctor flushed it out.

We live above a ramen shop in Ebisu. Our apartment is narrow and full of junk. Otousan always wanted to be an artist, and his canvases, paints and art books fill the living room and hallway. It drives my mother mad. I share a room with my older sister. Aoi's Gothic Lolita clothes, manga and make-up are everywhere, even on top of my keyboard.

'Yuki-chan? Are you awake?' she says.

I pull out my cockroach earplugs and put in my earphones to listen to YUKI. I love her, not just because we have the same name. She's different from the other pop stars. Her songs are deep. I listen to 'Nagai Yume'. Long Dream. It's about the baby she lost, and it's happy and sad at the same time. ٩(₀•‿•₀)۶ (╥_╥). The song eases me into a long, troubled dream of my own where I try to sneak out of fancy hotels without paying. It's a relief to wake up, but only for a second. The thought of going to school fills me with despair, so I text my friends. I put on my uniform, but instead of heading to class, I go to Hachiko and wait by the dog statue. A salaryman approaches with a furtive look.

'10,000 yen for your panties,' he says.

I turn away and look at my phone. Just then, Chie arrives.

'What did that oyaji want?' she says. I tell her.

'Get some cheap ones and keep them in your schoolbag. Easy money.'

'Yada,' I say.

'I'm going to.'

Someone covers my eyes from behind and startles me. Ari-chan drops her hands and screws up her nose at the salaryman, who is still hanging around, staring.

'Oyaji kusa,' she says pointedly in his direction. 凸(￣∧￣) Aria is different from the rest of us. She says what she thinks, probably because she's hāfu. People think it's rude, but I like it.

We go to Seibu to try on make-up. Ari-chan keeps watch while I slip a Bulgari perfume tester into my bag. Chie takes a Dior lipstick. After Ari-chan pockets a YSL concealer, we head to Yoyogi Park and smoke on the grass. o0o｡(´｡̀ ｡̀)y~~

'Yuki, genki?' Aria says. 'You look like a panda.'

'I didn't sleep well.'

'Kawaisō,' she says, and pats my arm. (╯_<｡)ヾ(´▽｀) She knows my home situation isn't great. She's had a hard time too. Her mother is gaijin and on top of that, batsu ichi: divorced, strike one.

I decide on an internet café in Harajuku that has super comfortable recliners for a nap, but I spot my father at the counter. I duck behind a fake tree before he can see me. |д･) He has his briefcase with him, but isn't wearing his suit. The sag of his face makes my shoulders slump. Neither of us are where we are supposed to be. I slip away and take the Yamanote loop line to nod off on the train for an hour.

When I get home, Okasan says there is no more money for piano lessons. Music is the only thing that makes life at home bearable. I put on my shortest school skirt and cutest striped tie, apply mascara and lip gloss and put a pink bow in my hair. I have a couple of things to do tonight. First, I need to steal some knickers to sell. Then I'm going to Akihabara to be an idol. I love to sing and dance. ♪ ♪ ♪ ヽ(´∀｀)ゞ

How hard can it be?

Akiba is like an otaku's bedroom, not that I've ever seen one. Girls my age dressed in maid outfits hand out flyers on every corner. Idols beam cute smiles from advertisements for live shows and merchandise. AK-47 is the most famous idol café in Tokyo. There are forty-seven girls in the group, and their pictures line an exterior wall next to the entrance. Minna genki de chō kawaii. I wonder if I'm cute enough to join. My piano teacher says I'm a good singer. Maybe I could even write songs to perform. I ask the girl at the counter about applying for a job. She has a high ponytail and pink glitter on her cheeks. She guides me to a booth.

'Wait here,' she says. 'The boss will see you shortly.'

I check out my surroundings. A blackboard has AK-47 news written in chalk. Whiteboards have messages from the idols with love hearts and smiley faces. 'Life only one time!' 'Get free!' 'Be my Akiba friend!' (●‿●)♡ Signed portraits of the idols look like school photos. I look like I belong here, in my school uniform. AK-47 pop songs blare at high volume, and images of the group flash across projected video on the back wall. I study their moves. I'm in a hiphop dance group with Aria and Chie and a bunch of other girls at school. Their choreography looks pretty easy for me to follow. Our stuff is much cooler and sexier. I check out the customers. Many wear AK-47 T-shirts, often customised with glitter and fabric paint. A couple of idols stop by each table, to shake hands and chat. The men are wide eyed and open mouthed. They look like children at Disneyland. One has brought a Louis Vuitton bag as a gift for his favourite, who squeals with delight \(≧▽≦)/ and bows deeply.

I'm feeling really envious, when a man approaches.

'Yuki-san?' he asks. I nod, and stand up. He presents me his meishi: 'Jun Nakahashi, AK-47 Talent Manager'. He looks me up and down, and makes me spin around before we sit down.

'You have a pimple,' he says, and points at my chin. 'You're definitely cute, but you could lose a few pounds. The fans love slim girls with tiny waists. See Chieko over there. She used to be a bit chubby like you, but I put her on a strict diet. She's one of our most popular idols now. How old are you?'

'Sixteen.'

'You have a short window of opportunity to be a successful idol. Do you have any special talents?'

'I play piano, sing and write songs.'

'Excellent. Can you start training tonight?'

'Of course.'

He leads me to his office, where he shows me a long list of rules.

'You'll have to train and then audition to become a member of AK-47. Training is unpaid, but you can make money working in the café. It's a good way to observe the fans and see what they like. You won't have any free time, and you'll have to do everything I say; got that?'

'Hai!'

'You'll need to keep a food diary. Write down everything you eat and report to me. Get on these scales, that's a good girl, so I can track your progress. Yappari, you need to lose 3 kilos. No bread, desserts or candy, understood?'

'Hai!'

'This is very hard work, and you must remember: treat the fans like kings. They spend a lot of money and time on idols, as this is the most important thing in their lives. They are otaku so they don't have their own families or many friends. You must always be happy and bright, no matter how tired you are. Get their meishi, remember their names, so that they come back to the café. If you give good service and they like you, they will become your best supporters when you become an idol.'

A tall girl with rosy cheeks comes to the door.

'Ah, one of our top idols! Chieko is ranked number three in AK-47.'

I bow.

'Chieko, show the new girl around, please.'

I follow Chieko as she leads me to the rehearsal space, and then the dressing room, where I am to choose a locker.

'The fans really like you,' I say.

'Hontō ni, kodomo mitai,' she said. 'They are like my children. Without them, I'd be nothing.'

I beam at myself in the mirror, and try to wink in a super kawaii way.

'You have to work on your smile,' says Chieko. 'It's not heartfelt enough.'

Otousan still dresses and leaves for work in the mornings. I wonder how long he can keep this up. Knowing his secret makes him seem smaller. Okaasan is so stressed she doesn't notice that I am home late every night. Or maybe she just doesn't care. One less person in this tiny apartment to have to deal with. I will eventually have to tell her about my new job, but for now I am happy that I can pay for my weekly piano lesson.

'Karaoke, ikō!'

It's Ari-chan on the phone.

'I want to, but I can't.'

I feel torn. I miss my friends.

'We never see you these days.'

'Shōganai yo. I have to work hard.'

'But why do you want to be an idol? What's so great about it? Aren't the customers creepy?'

'The fans are nice to us. They're just lonely. I'm on café duty tonight. Stop by for a milkshake.'

Ari-chan strolls in to the café around six, and is immediately spotted by my boss.

'So who's this?' he asks. 'Me, ōki ne.'

Nakahashi-san is behaving like a fan, intrigued by Aria's large eyes. It's a bit weird. 'Why are your eyes so big? Are you hāfu?'

'Hai, sō desu,' says Ari-chan, smiling brightly. I know she hates people asking her that.

'What country? Amerika?'

'Nyū Jīrando.'

His eyes nearly pop out of his head. 'Eh! I love you, I want you, I need you,' he says, in English.

I can tell Aria hates him, but she accepts his meishi with a smile and a bow. He instructs me to order her any dessert she wants, on the house, before finally leaving us alone.

'How embarrassing,' she says. 'And what a weird thing for him to say.'

'Probably trying to impress you by speaking English.'

'Aren't you going to have dessert too?'

'I can't. I'm working. Anyway I'm not allowed to.'

Two customers sitting at the nearest table smile and wave at me. (*°-°)/(*°-°)/ They both wear spectacles and have shiny faces. I remember meeting one of them the other day. His name is Masu, and he works at a software company. He must be in his late thirties.

'Hello Yuki-chan!' he says.

I excuse myself to go speak to him.

'So how is it being a new face?' says Masu. 'You know, I came today especially to see you.'

'Arigatō gozaimasu! I'm so glad to see you. It's been great!'

He introduces me to his friend.

'This is the beautiful girl I was telling you about. We have to vote for her to be a new member.'

They both vow to support my budding career as an idol in any way they can ٩(₀˙▿˙₀)۶.

It's really nice they've taken an interest in me.

That night when I get home, my parents are arguing.

'I know you lost your job,' says Okaasan.

'I've been looking for another one.'

'If you can't provide, what use are you?'

I hear Otousan cry, and I want to feel sorry for him but I can't. I leave without them realising I'd even been home at all. I catch the train to Shibuya to buy some cute accessories for work. Outside Marui, a salaryman offers me 50,000 yen for something that doesn't sound so bad.

Love Hotel

After spending the day shut in his room playing video games, Keiji, thirty-five, arrived for his night shift at Hotel Blue Moon.

Here, discretion is paramount. After entering an obscured entrance, guests could select one of the themed rooms by simply pushing a button. All Keiji had to do was pass the keycard through a narrow slot. The lack of face time suited Keiji just fine. He could read his erotic manga in peace.

Keiji bounced into the cluttered office. Hiro looked up from his instant ramen and said, 'Hey, nerd. Why are you so genki today?'

Keiji pointed to a small box he'd brought with him, which he opened to reveal a digital alarm clock. 'Eh?' said Hiro, unimpressed. Twenty-something, with spiky hair like a *Dragon Ball Z* character, Hiro looked down on a pudgy otaku like Keiji.

'Wait a second …' Keiji said.

He opened his laptop and darted out of the office. Hiro glanced over at a black window on the laptop screen. A video image of Keiji giving a thumbs-up in Room 11 appeared and startled Hiro, who nearly choked on his noodles.

* * *

Keiji and Hiro sat side by side and stared at the screen showing Room 11. Hiro's shift had finished, but he wasn't going anywhere. Room 11 was a candy-coloured extravaganza, a shrine to the kitten with no mouth. The pink and red room had a karaoke station, a heart-shaped jacuzzi and pink fur-lined handcuffs dangling from the ceiling at the foot of a round bed. There was a giant plushie next to a fluffy pink sofa, and plastic figurines of a popular feline character everywhere.

A salaryman with greying hair entered the room, followed by a girl in a high school uniform, a Louis Vuitton bag slung over her shoulder.

Keiji turned up the volume, and Hiro leaned forward.

The salaryman put down his briefcase and sat awkwardly on the sofa. The schoolgirl wore heavy eyeliner and had straight, dyed brown hair that she let fall like a glossy curtain between herself and the man. Her tiny rosebud mouth pouted as she scrolled through her pink phone.

The salaryman cleared his throat.

'Where do you live?'

'Near here,' the girl said without looking up.

'Do you like school?'

She shot him a scornful look.

'So …what are your hobbies?' he asked.

'Shopping,' said the girl. 'Designer brands only. Maybe we could go together. Can you take my picture?'

She held out her phone and put her little wrists through the handcuffs, sticking her arms out straight towards the lens, and flashed two V signs, smiling.

'Chīzu,' said the salaryman. 'So … that thing we talked about … what I asked you to do for me. Is it okay?'

The schoolgirl gave a stiff little nod and sat on the bed. He took off his glasses and positioned himself in her lap. She cradled him like a baby.

Keiji looked at Hiro.

'Maza-con?' said Hiro.

'Surely he'd go for an older woman then?' replied Keiji.

'And the fool just lies there.'

'Weirdo.'

They stopped watching, and played games on their phones. The schoolgirl and the salaryman sat there for an hour, a pietà in candy land.

* * *

By now it was 7.30 p.m. After a cursory going over by the cleaner, Room 11 was ready for new guests. A blonde in head-to-toe Dolce and Gabbana leopard print teetered into view on the arm of a man with slicked-back hair, dressed in a flashy suit with a purple paisley tie. He wore expensive-looking rings on both hands.

'Yakuza?' wondered Keiji.

'Can't wait to see her tits,' said Hiro.

The woman mixed a couple of Jack and Cokes, while the man sat down on the sofa and loosened his tie. Eyeing the room and the huge soft toy next to him, he declared, 'I hate this stuff.'

He spoke English well, with a British accent, in a voice thick with cigarettes and too much whiskey.

'Oh come on, Masa, I love it!' said the woman. 'You don't see shit like this in Sydney.'

'You wanna sing something, Cherry-chan?' he said, passing over a gold microphone and flicking on the karaoke machine.

'This one, by Britney Spears!' squealed Cherry. 'It's my favourite song to work out to.'

Masa keyed in it with some difficulty; finally, a squelchy bass line thumped out of the speakers.

Cherry recited the lyrics that scrolled across the TV screen while she stalked around the room, picking up and stroking the soft toys and figurines. She opened up what looked like a mini fridge; instead of bottles of booze, it housed rows of vibrators. She pulled out a rabbit model and a gigantic black dildo, and held them up with an arched eyebrow.

'No, no, Cherry … I have to pay for any you take out,' protested Masa, as she brandished another shaped like a corn cob. Throwing the sex toys on the bed, she leaned over to give him a good look down her cleavage, then perched on his knee and sang off key, getting the lyrics wrong. Masa winced.

'I fucking love this song!' Cherry cried. She turned her back to him. She peeled the top of her dress down slowly with one hand, revealing a pert rear in a lacy G-string. Her other taloned hand still clutched the microphone. She eased the dress slowly down her thighs. As the music built to a crescendo, Cherry stretched out her arms like a cabaret singer, getting ready for the big reveal.

She spun around and displayed her massive implants. Masa was slumped forward in his seat, passed out.

'Nice boobs,' said Hiro.

They watched as Cherry drew a dick on Masa's cheek with black eyeliner. She emptied the sex toy vending machine of its remaining wares and stuffed them all in her Louis Vuitton tote. They watched her contemplate relieving him of his Rolex, but she tossed it on the bed and left the room.

* * *

A middle-aged man and woman entered the room, both dressed in Cool Biz: casual business attire worn during Japan's unbearably humid summer months. The woman busied herself making green tea while the man sat down heavily and placed his head in his hands. She set a cup beside him and sat down.

'I think she knows,' he said. He let out a heavy sigh.

She nodded and bowed her head. 'It's getting harder for me at home too.'

'She complains that I'm not doing enough family service. Since my promotion I have so little time.'

A sole tear slid down her face. 'One last time then?' she asked.

'I'm just so tired. Gomen ne, Sayoko-chan,' he said.

They sat in silence and sipped their tea slowly. Finally, he put his hand over hers for a long moment. They helped each other with their coats and left.

*   *   *

Keiji looked at the clock. His shift would be over soon. Hiro had fallen asleep in his chair and was drooling.

A light flashed to indicate Room 11 had been selected. He handed the keys through the narrow slot and waited for the new guests to appear on screen. A young man led an exceptionally beautiful woman into the room. She wore a slinky black mini-dress, and her long legs were laced with satin ribbon. Her kittenish face was mesmerising. She smiled, showing very white teeth as she flipped her long black hair around. The man, cheekbones in a leather jacket, leaned back against the wall and watched her. *She's very tall*, thought Keiji. *Hey … isn't that …?*

'Hiro, wake up! Look!'

Hiro rubbed his eyes and wiped his mouth as he looked up at the screen.

'Holy shit!'

They watched as the two celebrities kissed and groped each other, before tumbling onto the round bed.

'This is great!' said Hiro. 'Aren't they both married to other people?'

The woman stood up and let her hair fall over her face. She bit her bottom lip and pulled her dress off.

'Flawless,' murmured Keiji.

'Now we're finally going to see some action!' said Hiro.

They high-fived each other.

She unhooked her bra and flung it straight ahead. The screen went black.

'Dammit!' said Hiro.

'Don't worry,' said Keiji. 'I have a back-up.'

Keiji switched on a second camera; it was hidden in a soft toy. A window opened up on screen: an arty looking shot of dark shadows rising and falling across pink wallpaper.

'It's pointing the wrong way!' Hiro said.

'We can still hear them,' said Keiji.

'Why would I want to listen to them? I'm not a creep. I'm outta here. Later, nerd.'

Keiji took some butter-flavoured Jagariko out of his backpack and crunched away as the couple's moans quickened. A brief silence was followed by a rustle of sheets and the rasp of a cigarette lighter.

'I love you,' the woman said.

'I don't blame you,' said the man, and zipped up his jeans.

How lucky, thought Keiji.

The Storm

Here we are, two young couples at a Michelin-starred restaurant in Aoyama, pretending to read the menu. The boys are traders at Barclays, us girls former dancers who once worked at the world's top-earning gentlemen's club in Roppongi. I don't know why we keep up this charade of being people who go out for nice dinners when all we want to do is *get on it*.

The predominately grey decor is punctuated by a baroque flower arrangement of bruised pink peonies, white roses and wild grapes. Vine leaves and tendrils trail across the table. I finally manage to focus on the swirly serif print in front of me.

'Do we have to do the degustation? It's eighteen courses.'

'This place was tough to get into,' says Jeff, my fiancé, and orders it for everyone.

'Who's got the baggie?' says Cindy, her green-gold eyes very wide, very frank.

A collective exhale. There, someone said it. Jeff nods, and Cindy reaches over to palm the coke from him. She's a platinum blonde; her strapless Herve Leger bandage dress accentuates delicate clavicles that glisten. Her husband, Will, a barrow boy from London made good, opens his mouth to say something, but she slinks off to the bathroom before he can.

The four of us are going to Bali next week. We hang out most weekends, and take lavish trips together. This year we've done Vegas, Palm Springs for Coachella, and Croatia.

Being a foreigner in Japan often means that (a) you are running away from your family (natch) and (b) you wind up being friends with people you wouldn't ordinarily be friends with (check). I'm not saying I don't like my friends. I love them. But I love them against my better judgement.

I excuse myself and join Cindy in the bathroom. She's smoothing the front of her dress down and frowning at the mirror.

'You can see my belly in this dress,' she says.

Said belly is non-existent. Cindy's abdomen is flat and taut, the result of a gruelling fitness regimen and rigid diet.

'You're beautiful,' I say, knowing she won't believe me. I hold my hand out for the drugs.

'At least you won't feel like eating now.'

The boys take their turn in the bathroom, and a brittle liveliness settles over the table. Waiters roll out an array of artful dishes with great ceremony, but nobody has any appetite.

The boys huddle to decide who will expense the bill. They herd Cindy and me into cabs while holding umbrellas over us in the light drizzle. The neon lights of Roppongi bleed across the windows.

A life-size statue of a Dobermann pinscher with its chest bound in intricate shibari knots guards an entrance under a backlit sign of a scarlet stiletto. Foreigners aren't usually allowed in this club, but the master has taken a shine to Jeff. My fiancé has classic good looks: strong jaw, angular face. The Japanese nurses were crazy for him when he was in hospital last year with a broken femur. I came to pick him up and discovered the hottest one on her knees, lacing a shoe on his good leg, gazing up at him with wet, adoring eyes.

Inside Sugar Heel, women in strappy bondage gear greet us. Well-heeled Japanese seated at shiny black booths and tables around a low stage watch a man in a shirt and tie getting his bare ass whipped by a dominatrix with shocking pink hair. As the cat o' nine tails cracks across his quivering buttocks, a hostess in a conical bra seats us at a booth behind a velvet rope. The master of the club, Abe-san, hurries over to offer Jeff a glass goblet bigger than Jeff's head. Jeff grips the thick stem and swirls the glass around, eyeing its pink contents. Abe-san tells us it's a cocktail made with habushu, snake liquor from Okinawa. Jeff takes a cautious sip, nods and then passes it around for us to try.

'It's pretty potent,' he says.

'Your son stand up!' says Abe-san.

A thin-faced woman in a leather collar approaches our table with a burning red candle.

'Dōzo,' she says, and gestures for Cindy to drip hot wax on her pointy tits.

'This place is bonkers,' says Will, dabbing his brow with an oshibori. 'Why haven't I been here before?'

'You were in Hong Kong last time,' says Cindy.

'Just so you know, Will,' I say. 'You have to have a vodka enema to be allowed to stay.' I point to the now empty stage. The businessman/whipping boy is drinking whiskey with a cute tattooed girl, his pants back on.

'You're not serious.'

I look at Jeff, who nods.

'We all had to do it our first time here. Right, Abe-san?' Jeff addresses the master, who is now perched next to him.

'Hai, sō desu Jeff-san! Everybody do vodka enema first time,' Abe-san says. 'Rule, desu node.'

'Wait, so you're telling me you did this too?' Will says to Cindy.

'Sure did, babe! This place is cool. No one cares.'

'Oh well. Here goes,' Will says.

Abe-san summons a hostess, who takes Will away to prepare. The pimp cup makes another circuit, and we slam a round of Jägermeister shots. Cindy leans forward, and I get a good look at her natural-looking fake tits. They are amazing, though she did once say she feels sad when she hugs me and my real boobs squish up against her.

A tiny woman in a latex bodystocking leads Will to the stage by a leash attached to a studded collar around his neck. Bare-chested, and wearing assless leather chaps, he's got a swagger on. He walks up to the stage bowlegged, like a cowboy. We all do a double take.

'He looks far too comfortable,' says Jeff.

'You might have to get him an outfit like that for home,' I say to Cindy, who, looking gobsmacked, mouths 'What the fuck.' Latex Woman bends Will over in front of the whole club. She is brandishing a large frosted glass syringe, and shows it to the crowd. We cheer loudly.

'Vodka enema yo!' she says, and casually slips it in Will's ass. That's when we get the laughs real bad. I literally cry. Will slowly straightens up like a punch-drunk boxer, and Latex grabs his hand and holds it up like a champion.

'He's so gullible,' says Cindy.

I stumble out of the aptly named Escobar to the unpleasant sound of crows cawing, and fish for my sunglasses. The sun rises too damn early in Japan.

We want to keep the party going, but we've had our fill of bars. Cindy and Will's is out, because their kid is at home with the nanny, so we head to the apartment I share with Jeff in Azabu Jūban. After a stop at the conbini to load up on Asahi beer and mixers, we take the side entrance to avoid the front desk, pile into the elevator and glide up to the thirty-sixth floor.

Our corner apartment has a panoramic view of the city. Shibuya to the west and the skyscrapers of Shinjuku to the east. The sky is streaked with pink and gold behind Mount Fuji in the distance. It's going to be a beautiful day. I lean over a dinner plate of fat lines with a rolled-up ichiman note. I try the right nostril but it's blocked, so I sniff the biggest line using the side that still works.

The sky is once again gold and pink, and I don't know if it's sunset or sunrise. We've been YouTube DJing for hours now, and it's starting to get old.

'Guys, I'm fading. I can't keep going.'

Jeff and Cindy rack up more lines and talk about getting more.

Jeff puts on a straw fedora, his holiday hat, and starts chugging beer before we leave for the airport. As soon as we clear security, he makes a beeline for the nearest bar. We are the last to board our flight to Bali. He kicks my carry-on suitcase as I walk on ahead of him. The second time he orders two vodka sodas for himself, the flight attendant cuts him off. He tries to argue, but she threatens to speak with the captain. Mercifully he settles down and passes out. I knock myself out with a Xanax.

The chaotic, dusty airport at Denpasar is a drag, and it's a relief to get into our air-conditioned car and be driven away from the choked central roads to a scenic part of the island. Jeff doesn't recall his Narita meltdown, and I don't remind him. It's a sweltering, hazy day. When we arrive at our hotel, we're given flutes of champagne and cold towels wrapped around woody stalks of freshly cut lemongrass. Our villa has a formal lounge area, with striped sofas and a large tapestry of a ram. The open-air his/her showers are lined with bamboo. We immediately strip off and have sex under the rainshower heads. It feels good to wash off the plane and dust and sex and get dressed. Jeff hands me a shiny black box.

'For you,' he says.

'It's not my birthday.'

I eye him with mock suspicion and open the box. It's a Bulgari necklace. A rose-gold snake pendant with green eyes. Jeff pulls me on to his lap.

'I love it,' I say, and wrap my arms around his neck.

'You deserve it,' he says. 'Okay; let's go find those two dummies.'

Cindy and Will are lounging around in the main hangout area of the compound. It's an open-air pavilion on the cliff's edge, with a backdrop of an infinity pool and the Indian Ocean. Will holds up a white business card that says 'I ♥ MUSHROOM' in the iconic 'I ♥ NY' font.

'Got this in Kuta from some locals,' he says. 'They deliver, twenty-four hours.'

'What are we waiting for?' said Jeff. 'Call 'em.'

The dealer pulls up on a moped. Without getting off, he hands Will a two-litre bottle of murky liquid in exchange for a fistful of rupees. We go back to our cliffside hangout and gather round. Will solemnly pours out a generous dose for each of us. My stomach turns just looking at it. It smells like funky wet dirt.

'Kampāi!'

I brace myself and tip the foul liquid down my throat. I manage to get it down in one gulp. My mouth and tongue turn numb. I chase it with a shot of Grey Goose, and let out a deep shudder.

Everyone has downed theirs except Cindy, who takes tiny sips and makes a face after each one.

It's the golden hour, and the temperature has cooled to a pleasant level. A light breeze wafts through the open sides of the pavilion, carrying with it distant music that sounds like wind chimes, gently struck bamboo and clocks ticking. A gamelan orchestra seems to be ever present on this island, shimmering away in the undergrowth and the vines.

We each find a comfortable spot to wait for the mushrooms to kick in. Cindy and Will lie next to each other in a hammock and swing lazily back and forth. Jeff and I sprawl out on the banquette seating. A friend who lives on the island, a DJ called Taro, arrives with some Brazilian chick, and they set up some decks. When they're done, he perches on one of the black plastic sixties' chairs at the bar. They don't fit the rest of the decor.

'You look like you're at the hairdressers,' says Will, and everyone finds this way too funny. Taro spins some deep house. The beat is hypnotic, and everyone is quiet.

'Are you feeling it?' says Cindy to me, her eyes sparkling in the half light, pupils dilated.

I feel as if my entire head is opening up and folding over on itself. Cindy's flouncy dress leaves a cerise trail as she crosses the room. The sun slowly melts into the ocean and turns the golden sky indigo. I hear the gamelan again, louder now, the sound of water running over stones, people sighing in the next resort over. I close my eyes and see a grid pattern, oscillating neon colours over black, and when I open them again I see this momentarily like a web over everything.

I dip my toes in the pool. The water feels thick, like jelly.

'Come and feel the water,' I say, and Cindy and Will join me, trailing their fingers in the goop. Taro's friend Karen appears. I didn't take any notice of her before. Her movements are contained and graceful. She sheds her sundress to reveal a sleek black bathing suit and dives in. She comes up for air, black hair wet against her skull, and she has morphed into a baby seal. Her hands clap like flippers, and she has long shiny whiskers around her maw.

'Why don't you come in,' she says in her husky seal voice. I hesitate for a second before stripping down to my bikini and diving in at the deep end.

'It's nice in here,' she says, and her fingers brush against my nipple accidentally. Her touch radiates through my breast, and I stare at her. Someone grabs me by my waist, and it's Cindy bobbing in the water behind me. She takes my hands and pulls me through the water. Droplets of water on her shoulder blades glitter and refract like jewels.

She turns to smile at me, and her teeth are so white they are blinding. Karen glides over and the three of us roll around in the water.

'You're so pretty,' says Karen, and gives me a fierce little kiss. It takes me by surprise. My teeth bash into hers, and we both laugh. I glance up and see Jeff and Will looking at us, the lit ends of their cigarettes glowing in the dark.

The night air feels thin after the jelly water. Maybe this is what leaving the womb feels like. Cold and unsupported. I wrap myself up in a thick towel and pad off to the bathroom. The statues watch me; their heads twist and turn in unnatural positions as I pass by. I sit on the toilet and piss for what seems like a really long time. Eons pass; civilisations rise and fall. I'm mesmerised by a painting of an Indonesian dancer in traditional dress. She is blue and green and gold with long silver nails. She turns her head and sighs, and I sigh too, and then I have a sudden urge to throw up. I leap up and puke stars and rainbows into the bowl. I purge old fears and anxieties that have been resting in my gut. They pour out of my mouth rejiggered as beauty. The puking goes on and on, until there's nothing left. I sit there on the floor clutching the bowl. I hear the others clinking their glasses and laughing outside and feel pathetic. I will myself to stand up and walk over to the mirror. As soon as I look at my reflection I realise it is a mistake. My skin is blotchy and discoloured, covered with green and purple scales that shimmer and move. I shiver and walk back past the watching statues to join the others. Jeff is saying that you should never look at your penis when you're tripping: he did once, and it had the face of his dead grandfather.

The phone behind the bar rings, and we all look at it like it's a tarantula.

'Don't answer it,' I say.

It rings and rings until Jeff picks it up.

'That was the front desk. There's a storm coming,' he says.

The light breeze from before has picked up in intensity without us noticing. All around, leaves are rustling, and, as if on cue, the palm trees start to swing from side to side. The boys unroll the canvas awnings on all four sides of the open pavilion. A low rumble of thunder, followed by a loud crack of lightning and then a deluge of tropical rain hits hard and fast. It falls in diagonal sheets. I've never seen rain so heavy before. Taro turns up the music so we can hear it over the rain. The track playing has a sample from The Doors, some refrain about it being the end, friends. A bright orange crab scuttles in for shelter. A couple of frogs leap in under the awning. Even a lime-green snake slithers in and startles Jeff, who tries to stamp on it.

'Don't kill it!' I shout. He tries to stomp on it again.

The peak of the trip passes with the storm. The next few hours are the usual blur of drinks, cigarettes and talking shit. I get into a deep and meaningful with Taro about the expat bubble in Tokyo and the idea of the money hose: if you have a problem, just get the money hose and wash that shit away. Around midnight, I stumble to the bathroom. I hear giggling. The door creaks opens and Cindy pops a dishevelled head out to peer around it.

'Oh hey,' she says, and opens the door to reveal Jeff behind her.

'I was just giving Cindy a line,' he says.

*   *   *

'You're a fit bird,' says the ageing rock star, strutting around the hotel room with a towel around his waist. We'd met at a bar earlier in the evening.

'I don't usually do this.'

He looked at me.

'My fiancé shagged my best friend.'

'Ah … poor bunny. You're a top bird. Boys will be boys, eh.'

He gives my new tits a squeeze. They still feel a bit numb. I got them done in Phuket. I feel really good about them.

Mama

After considerable snooping, Tania discovered that her husband had been having an affair. Furious at being found out, Niko took Tania's Japanese chef knife, the special one with her name engraved on the blade, and threatened to kill himself if she left him. Tania promptly went on a bender and hooked up with a professional baseball player.

Upon her return to the marital home, Niko's elderly parents confronted her. Why was she threatening to leave their son and shame the family? Tania showed them the photos she'd found online. Niko clutching a chubby blonde in a neon mesh outfit at a nightclub. Supposedly away on business, he'd taken this woman on a holiday in Europe. Niko's mother, a perpetually disappointed woman, scoffed and said: 'They all do it. Even Otousan did it.'

Tania turned and stared at Niko's dad, a kind man who looked like a Japanese Father Christmas. He nodded mournfully, on the verge of tears.

'I did; it's true. Please don't get a divorce.'

But she left Niko anyway. Now she was on her own in Tokyo and broke.

Tania began working for a caterer, selling lunches to office workers in the mornings, but she needed more money, and fast. Tania called Iraqi Lisa.

'There's a hostess club in Ginza I used to work at,' said Lisa. 'You get paid at the end of every night. The Mama-san is Chinese. Tell her I sent you.'

Tania wasn't keen on drinking with old men every night, but one day she found herself disembarking at Ginza station.

She hadn't spent much time in this part of town. The luxury shops, bars and restaurants of Ginza catered for an older, well-heeled crowd. Ginza was where her now-former mother-in-law shopped for Ferragamo shoes and had lunch with her friends. Tania stopped to marvel at a 150-year-old Japanese maple bonsai in a shop window. Its twisted trunk and limbs were offset by a cascade of delicate red leaves. Gnarled roots pushed up through a mound of velvety green moss in fine porcelain. It was breathtaking, and so was the price: 1.5 million yen.

Tania found the club tucked away on a side street. A willowy Chinese woman opened the door distractedly and looked her up and down while puffing on a cigarillo, before waving her in with an air of 'you'll do, I suppose.'

The club was very small, with only four tables, a bar brightly lit in the corner and a karaoke machine. The Mama-san motioned for Tania to sit down. She wore a gold Cartier watch, a powder-blue slip dress and low kitten heels. Tania guessed she was pushing fifty. She was an attractive woman with watchful eyes in a smooth, oval face. Tania thought she must have been very beautiful in her youth. She still was.

'What country?' said the woman brusquely, taking a long drag and squinting through the smoke.

'New Zealand.'

'Not Australia?'

Tania shook her head.

'Are you sure? Australian girls very lazy! I don't need lazy girls here! I am Bei, but you call me Mama.'

'Hajimemashite, Mama-san.'

'You speak Japanese? Good, good! Oh kay, you work tonight? You change in toilet.'

The toilet had a worn pink candlewick cover on the seat. Tania wondered how often it got washed. Iraqi Lisa had told her she'd be put to work immediately, so she was already made up and had a cheap cocktail dress in her backpack. She pulled it on quickly to avoid spending time in the unpleasant toilet/dressing room. She was ready.

Two grey-haired customers entered the club, their overcoats slick with rain. Mama barked out orders.

'Uwagi!'

Tania rushed to help them with their wet coats and briefcases.

'Oshibori!'

Tania held out a heated towel to one of the men, who grabbed it without looking at her and wiped his face.

'Haizara!'

Tania grabbed an ashtray from the bar and placed it next to her customer as he pulled out a cigarette.

'Matchi!'

Tania held out a light.

'Onomimono!'

She added ice to tumblers and mixed their drinks.

'Hello, hello! Long time no see, ne!' Mama's beaming smile flooded the room.

Over the next few weeks, Tania became adept at responding to and anticipating Mama's frequent commands. Another key requirement was to be genki. Mama was an expert at it: she was the life of the party.

She gently poked fun at her guests while showering them with affection and flattery. She deftly massaged shoulders and egos. She plonked herself in laps and played drinking games. She sang Japanese enka while draped over the peach velvet furniture. Her favourite song mourned the transience of female beauty.

Before her misty-eyed customers could cry into their drinks and call out, 'Mama, you're still the most beautiful!' she'd crack a filthy joke and have them in hysterics. Mama had known most of her customers for years. She'd once been a hostess too, and had become successful enough to open her own club.

Every night before the club opened, Mama sent Tania out to buy bottles of Scotch and snacks. Tania loved weaving through the narrow alleyways, catching glimpses of women in kimono clacking along the cobblestones in their zori, sushi chefs laden with trays of shiny fresh fish and flashes of noren fluttering in doorways. It would suddenly hit her. How did she end up here? When she first arrived in Tokyo, everything was weird. Then it became normal. Now it was weird that it was normal.

As Tania picked out ripe mangoes for the customers, she daydreamed about being rich, and thought about how she'd buy herself a navy Chanel 2.55 bag.

Mama sat in the corner and smoked furiously, with one eye on the clock. It was already 9.30 p.m. Tania sat with the other two hostesses, Agatha from Poland and Lucia from Lithuania, anxious about Mama's foul mood.

'No customer, but I still pay you every hour,' Mama said. She stubbed out her cigarette. 'Okay, this too boring. Let's make Happy Friday.' She fished out a plastic shopping bag and a deck of cards from behind the bar. She tipped out the contents of the bag: lacy, barely there G-strings.

'I buy in China. You play Mama. If you win, you get,' she said, pointing to the pile of lingerie.

'And if Mama wins?' asked Lucia.

'Just for fun, ne,' said Mama. She dealt a round of poker.

Tania picked up her hand and saw that every card had a different naked man on it, each with a huge penis, eighties' hair and tan-lines.

'Look at this one,' Agatha said, showing them her King of Hearts, a bodybuilder in cut-off denim shorts with a raging erection poking out through the leg. The women cackled in unison.

Tania was winning. She picked out a white lacy pair that tied at the sides, a hot pink thong with a strand of pearls instead of a fabric gusset and a red crotchless number.

'You good at poker, ne,' said Mama. 'Your boyfriend have Happy Friday too.'

'I don't have a boyfriend. I'm getting a divorce.'

'Omedetō,' Mama said.

'Do you have a boyfriend, Mama?' asked Lucia.

'Yes,' Mama said, 'but they're all married.'

Lucia eyed Tania's pile of winnings.

'It's not fair that we don't have prizes for you, Mama,' she said.

'Just for fun, ne,' said Mama.

'Come on, Mama, let's make it interesting,' said Agatha.

'Okay. Next winner plays me,' Mama said.

Tania continued her streak and won the next hand. Mama looked pleased.

'Okay, just me and you now, ne. If you win, you get 50,000 yen. If I win ...' Mama made a big show of thinking hard. 'Hmm, what do I want, Tania-chan? What do I need, ne?'

Tania started to feel nervous. 'Just for fun, right?'

'Yes, yes, of course, yo! This fun!' Mama's smile grew. 'Oh I know! Mama have very good idea! I need Chi-Mama.'

'What do you mean?' asked Tania.

'I have club in Shanghai. If I win, you be my Chi-Mama. You go Shanghai and run my club.'

'Woah, I don't know ...'

Tania had never been to China. However, she could do with 50,000 yen if she won.

She looked over at Agatha and Lucia.

'Good chance!' said Agatha.

Kōhine

* * *

It was Friday night. Two new girls had come into the club: Nicole from Canada and Bianca from Brazil.

'You can call me Mama,' said Tania, admiring the way her new Rolex gleamed on her wrist.

Leaping-off Place I

I called Mum to see if she was gonna be home on New Year's Eve and of course she was going out, so I was free to do whatever.

I called all my friends. Everyone liked hanging out at my place because we lived in Daikanyama. It's a very fashionable area with cool shops and cute cafés. People were always surprised and envious that we lived in such a fancy part of Tokyo.

Masaya arrived first. He was dressed in black, and his dyed red hair hung in his eyes, as usual. He looked so cool. He held out a giant Spongebob Squarepants soft toy.

'Suponji bobu daisuki, arigatō!' I said, and hugged him and Spongebob tight.

Masaya and I met a year earlier, on our first day at Sakura High. Masaya's mum insisted that he take a picture with 'that really cute girl'. I often teased him about his bright red cheeks in the photo.

Pin-pon! My friends were at the door, clutching snacks and booze.

'Ari-chan, genki?'

'Happy New Year!'

'Ojama shimāsu!'

'Look at Yuki's new hair!'

'Kawaii!'

'Who wants a chu-hi?' Yuki said, handing out cans of peach shochu. We each cracked one open and said, 'Kampāi'.

Us girls were in a hiphop dance group, so we practised some of our moves. We were having fun, listening to music and goofing around. Then Chie opened a bottle of something strong, and we took turns swigging from it. It was sickly sweet. I don't remember things clearly after that. I threw up. Then Masaya's mother called and said he had to go home, right away.

'Your mum never cared about you being home before.'

'New Year dakara.'

Masaya usually spent a lot of time at my place because he didn't get along with his mum. She was a single mother like mine, which is pretty weird in Japan. Masaya was always hungry and broke, so Mum would give me extra cash so he could have pocket money like I did. Having him around made her feel less guilty about working all the time. Or drinking, when she wasn't working.

'You can't go!'

'I have to.'

'Don't leave me by myself!'

I wasn't normally like this, but I'd never been drunk before. I kept tripping over and bumping into things. The argument went on and on, and the six of us spilled out on to the back balcony. Masaya's phone started up again.

'She's angry,' Masaya said. 'I really have to leave now.'

I climbed up on to the railing.

'No,' I said. Why wasn't he listening to me?

All my friends freaked out.

'Ari-chan, what are you doing?'

'Please get down!'

'Abunai-tteba!'

'Yada!' Yuki started crying.

When I was ten, I'd faked an asthma attack over the phone so Mum would come home early from work. She'd rushed back in a panic. When she realised I wasn't sick, she was furious. She didn't understand how lonely I was.

Two crows were sitting in the tree across from our balcony, watching me.

'Ari-chan, please get down! I'm scared!' said Masaya.

'You can't go,' I said.

'I love you! Stop this!'

'You can't leave me.'

I hate being left. I was always being left. So I left him. I left everyone.

I was floating above everything. I could see my body on the ground, four floors down in our neighbour's yard. My leg was twisted back in an awkward position, from where I'd hit the fence on the way down. My head was bleeding, all over my favourite hoodie. My friends cried as the ambulance officers worked on my body. Masaya sat against the back fence and stared straight ahead like a zombie.

Dying hurt. I don't recommend it. It sucked. Then there was a freezing cold, dark place. It was too cramped and lonely and gave me the creeps, so I left. Whoosh, just like that. High above the city, I could see everything.

I wandered around Shibuya. I knew these streets well, but I was so lost.

I was eight years old again; the age I was when I first came to Japan. I bumped into my mother's ex-husband on Meiji Dori Avenue. He was his younger self too. He looked just like Bruce Lee. He paled when he saw me.

'You look like you've seen a ghost,' I said.

Dai grabbed me by the shoulders. He looked at me for a long time.

'Why?' he finally managed to say.

'I don't know.'

I tried to keep my distance from Mum.

I saw her outside our apartment, dressed in black.

'I'm so sorry, Mum! I didn't mean it!'

Later that day, she nearly saw me sitting next to her in a taxi, but her hand reached for mine and found nothing.

I was constructing an intricate arrangement of origami cranes when Yuki saw me, in a dream. Yuki was all perfect looking, like a doll. Her eyes opened wide beneath her blunt bangs.

'Ari-chan, what are you doing?' she asked, as I concentrated on a particularly tricky part.

'I'm making a house for me and Masaya in New Zealand. Please tell him to stop crying.'

Playgrounds in Tokyo look like they belong in horror movies. The equipment is rusty and faded and there's never any grass. Just concrete. I went to the one near my house and sat in a swing. I wished I could have a cigarette. I started smoking a couple of months ago. Mum didn't know about that. I swung back and forth trying to make the swing creak in a creepy way when a black cat jumped up on my lap.

I tried to stroke its fur, but I couldn't feel anything, so I pushed it off. It hissed at me like a snake.

I didn't know where to go, so I went home. I couldn't avoid Mum forever.

She was going through my things. She'd hold something like my pink comb, or the perfume I got from Disneyland, and cry over it.

'That's just crap from the 100-yen shop,' I said. 'And you hate Disneyland.'

It was pointless because she couldn't hear me. She never listened anyway.

Mum found a letter that I wrote to the wrestler Eddie Guerrero when he died. When I was younger, I really loved wrestling. I would try to talk to her about it but she wasn't interested.

'You know it's fake, right?' she'd say.

'I don't care; it's my stress release.'

Mum left me with Nana in New Zealand for ages when she first went to Japan. Then she told me on the phone she was getting married to some Japanese guy I'd never met. Dai turned out to be mostly okay, but still.

It didn't last. He wasn't ready to get married. Even I could have told her that.

Mum never had to move countries and learn a new language like me. Being a kid really sucks most of the time. You have to go along with whatever adults decide.

Leaping-off Place I

She read my letter aloud:

Dear Eddie,
I'm really sad that you're gone. When I first heard the news, I found it hard to believe. I tried to convince myself that it was a joke. But deep down I knew it wasn't. But I just couldn't understand why a man full of life could just disappear like that. I mean, I had just saw you wrestle on TV a couple of days ago and now you're gone? I still find it hard to face what has happened. I know you wouldn't want your fans and your loved ones to cry over your death, but I just want you to know that everyone misses you. SmackDown isn't the same without you! I haven't watched SmackDown since you died. It just breaks my heart to see all your fellow wrestlers crying and stuff. My favourite memory of you is the time that you tried to sell Kurt Angle's personal stuff. That was so funny! You had a sense of humour like no other and I have so many funny memories of you! I also liked the angle when you soaked the Big Show in raw sewage! That's another good one. Anyway, goodbye Eddie. Everybody misses you!

Mum was an ugly crier. Her face went all blotchy.

'That wasn't written to you! It's private! Stop going through all my stuff!' I said.

The sobbing stopped abruptly. She had an odd look on her face.

'Can you hear me? Mum?'

Then I realised she was holding the pack of Marlboro Lights I'd hidden in one of my socks. Busted. I hoped she wouldn't find my condoms too.

I went to Shibuya to visit my old haunts. Get it? Lol. I went to my favourite purikura. You know, those really great photo sticker booths they have in Japan. None of my friends were there. They were all too sad to go. I wouldn't have shown up in the photos anyway.

I drifted down to Shibuya Crossing. It's the big scramble crossing you see in time-lapse footage of Tokyo. People scurrying back and forth like ants beneath giant TV screens. I was standing on the kerb waiting for the cross signal when I remembered something I had said to Mum in that exact same spot:

'I feel like if I dropped down dead right here, no one would care and people would just walk right over me.'

Mum looked at me. I had her full attention, for once.

'I know exactly what you mean,' she said.

I stood right in the middle of the crossing, and let the crowds of people pass through me. No one noticed, except for a girl with pink hair. I saw her shiver.

I floated over to Harajuku, past Condomania. I remembered the first time I saw that shop. I was nine.

Seeing the giant smiling yellow banana on the facade, I pulled on Mum's arm and said:

'Can we go to the banana shop? Pleeease?'

'Aria, that's not a banana. It's a condom.'

'What's that?'

'Men wear them on their penis during sex to stop getting women pregnant and prevent disease.'

'But why would people have sex if they don't want to make a baby?'

But when she explained, I covered my ears.

'I wish you hadn't told me!' I wailed.

Mum tried not to laugh.

The smell of freshly made crepes wafted down the street from Angel's Heart on Takeshita Dori. I watched as the server loaded a crepe with dollops of custard, fresh strawberries and whipped cream before drizzling chocolate sauce all over that deliciousness. That's when I really started to regret dying. I was so hungry.

I looked through the windows at Shakey's Pizza. It was the lunch buffet. I went all the time with my friends. Clusters of high school students lounged around in booths, laughing and stuffing themselves with all-you-can-eat pizza. I stood outside and watched.

* * *

Something is pulling me. Like a thread. I am being pulled away. Far, far away across the seas. Back to where I belong. Like a fish on a hook.

I want to see Tokyo one last time.

I get on the giant ferris wheel in Odaiba. I ride it up, up, up to the top and take it all in. That big patch of green over there is Yoyogi Park; the grey field of stone, Aoyama Cemetery. Where the dead live. Tokyo Tower, orange like a traffic cone. Shibuya 109! Tokyo Bay. And Fuji-san watches over it all.

Long golden minutes turn to night, and the city lights and neon signs come alive. Tokyo is so much prettier at night. Like a geisha. Transformed.

Crows swoop and caw around me. I listen to them talk.

'Look at that flightless,' one says. 'Is she lost?'

'She needs to go that way,' says another, and cocks its head south-west.

Hot summers in the city. It's festival time, and paper lanterns float above the streets. Fat toro sushi. So pink and fresh it glistens.

Under the lights at our first concert: Chie, Yuki and I. We are late because someone jumped on the train tracks. I'm wearing Mum's long suede boots. At school clean-up, Yamasaki-sensei puts on 'Sex Bomb' by Tom Jones over the public address system. Kids dance around with brooms and feather dusters and fall about laughing. Smile, chīzu! Here we are at Tokyo Disneyland. My favourite ride – It's a

Small World After All. There are two tiny Māori dolls in the display, which I always look for as I float past. If you blink, you'll miss them. New Zealand is so far away. I dream in Japanese now. At junior high graduation, Mum takes my photo under a cherry blossom tree in full bloom. The breeze makes the blossoms fall like rain and they catch in my hair.

Sayonara.

The Void

The bar is tucked away behind a shrine in Shibuya, and its graffittied doors don't swing open until well after midnight. Inside its blood-red walls, crystal chandeliers drip from the ceiling and a stag's head casts a dead eye over hip Japanese and gaijin. A bald man with a handlebar moustache stands at the bar, dressed in black. His dark eyes dart around the room.

'I love this place,' he says to the two women who've just joined him, Hiromi and Maia.

'This is my friend, the Director,' says Hiromi. 'He's making a movie here in Tokyo.' A second-generation

Korean, she has a geometric haircut and wears a Comme des Garçons suit.

'I met a crazy French guy here last night,' the Director says. 'I put him in my movie.'

'You cast a random you met in a bar?' says Maia. She is high on Columbian cocaine.

'Yes,' says the Director. 'One of the funniest people I've ever met in my life.'

'Wait – is his name Cyril? Quite tall; looks like a werewolf? Dresses rockabilly?' says Maia.

'Do you know him?'

'Yes! He's one of my best friends. We're in a band together. The Cyprines.'

The Director throws his head back and laughs.

'What's so funny?' said Hiromi.

'Cyprine means pussy juice in French,' says Maia.

A camera follows the Actress as she winds her way through the haze-filled club on to the packed dancefloor. Wearing tight gold pants and a string bikini top, her lithe body makes sexy, sinuous movements, but she is wobbly on her spindly heels. The Actress handed a brown paper bag to Maia when she first arrived.

'Stash this for me and don't tell anyone,' she said, and strode off with a conspiratorial wink before Maia had a chance to say anything. Maia put the bottle behind a bag at her feet. She was sitting with a group of teens in school uniform in the VIP area. When the Director discovered that Maia had a teenage daughter, he'd asked her to arrange for her daughter and ten of her friends to be extras in this club scene. It had been a little tricky: most Japanese parents would baulk at their kids hanging out with a bunch of strange foreigners in an Aoyama nightclub, but here they were. Aria looked like she could be Japanese, or at least a hafū. Years ago, Hiromi had told Maia to let people believe Aria was Japanese.

'Don't say anything about her being Māori. It'll be easier for her.'

Hiromi knew what she was talking about, having growing up Korean in Japan. Aria had moved to Japan at the age of eight, and now, at sixteen, spoke Japanese like a native. On her first day at school in Japan, one of the other kids kept pointing at her and saying 'Chigau-yo.' Chigau means different. It also means wrong.

A crew member ushers them on to the dancefloor to join the crowd.

After shooting finally wraps for the night, Cyril and the Director come over to Maia and Aria.

'Aria, come meet everyone,' the Director says. He takes her around the room and introduces her to all the actors and crew. Leggy and confident, Aria in her short check skirt and school tie is the centre of attention. A talent agent gives Maia his card.

'Your daughter is beautiful. Please call me.'

The wrap party is a blur. Maia does shots of habushu, with the Actress.

'You're an English teacher?' the Actress says to Maia. 'You don't seem like an English teacher. You look an artist.'

A group of them piles into a couple of cabs and goes back to the apartment where the Director is staying.

Maia sits on a sofa in the living room, away from the others in the kitchen She picks up a book on the coffee table, opens it to a random page and begins reading. She sits up and flips through the book, stopping in places to read passages aloud to herself, under her breath.

She slips the book into her handbag and leaves.

* * *

Maia sits on a zabuton cushion next to a shrine for Aria: photos, flowers, cards, candles and incense on a low table in the living room.

The Director visits.

'Do you know what my movie is about?' he says.

'No.'

'It's about someone dying in Tokyo, and their soul leaving the body. The camera has a bird's-eye view of this, the person looking down from above. It's based on *The Tibetan Book of the Dead*.'

Maia goes to her bedroom, and comes back holding a well-thumbed paperback in her hands.

'After the wrap party, I took this.'

It's *The Tibetan Book of the Dead*.

'Keep it. I had my editor put together all the footage we have of Aria,' he says. He hands her a DVD.

She watches Aria dancing in the club. The lights are shining on her.

Just Holden Together

Whenever Mum drove her mint cream 1974 Holden Kingswood into town, she would attract double takes as she rumbled around. A tiny brown lady who barely came up to my shoulder, she had to sit on a cushion to peer over the steering wheel. She looked like a child driving.

'Chur, that's a straight-as Holden,' Māori fullas would say. 'How much your old lady want for it?'

But the Holden wasn't for sale.

I stepped off the plane, and the stench of the nearby sewage ponds rose to greet me. I spotted Mum's whale of a car and went over. She got out and embraced me. Clad in winter woolies and gumboots, worry clouded her face.

'What's wrong, Mum?'

'It's about time you came home. Put your suitcase in the back.'

Rabbits darted across the road lined with pines, the trees' foliage horizontal strokes of yellow and green. The muddy river flowed past sluggish and slow as if powerful forces roiled beneath its surface. Perhaps a taniwha lurked in the deep.

The past is heavy, I thought.

Only if you hold on to it, said the imaginary Buddhist monk in my mind. An Australian called Zen Ken, he was always chiming in with his two cents.

Down the main drag I noticed there were even more vacant shops. A couple of locals lurched past, looking like extras from *The Walking Dead*. I sighed. Auckland seemed very far away.

We pulled into the driveway of Mum's place, a faded yellow villa with an overgrown garden.

'Girl, look at this,' Mum said, opening the boot.

A dirty bundle lay there. I flipped the folds back to reveal a sawn-off shotgun. I quickly withdrew my hand.

'That bloody brother of yours borrowed my car yesterday. Now I hear his mate has been arrested. What should I do with it?'

'We better go see him,' I said.

We drove over the river to my brother Tāne's house, another rundown villa. Māori carvings in varying states of completion were dotted amongst the flax bushes, and the wooden letterbox was shaped like a pātaka, the patterns drawn on with a Vivid. No one answered the front door, so we let ourselves in. Everything was upside down. Squabs had been pulled off the sofa, drawers emptied of their contents on to the floor and the furniture strewn around in disarray.

'Looks like the cops beat us to it,' I said, opening the back door. A large black rubbish bag sat in the middle of the yard, overflowing with marijuana buds. I went over and examined them. Sticky, pungent, purple heads.

Mum and I looked at each other.

'How did the cops miss that?' Mum said.

'They wouldn't think anyone would be stupid enough to leave a huge bag of weed sitting in their backyard.'

'What should we do?' Mum asked.

I picked up the bag and chucked it in the boot.

Mum said karakia and my younger brother, Matiu, and I tucked into big plates of boil-up: pork bones, pūhā, potatoes, kūmara and doughboys.

'I've been craving this,' I said, savouring the flavourful broth, its round richness cut by the sharp taste of the pūhā. I thickly buttered some parāoa takakau to sop up the juices.

'You used to turn your nose up at our kai,' Mum said.

'I still hate fish heads!'

They were Mum's favourite. She loved to suck the eyes out and show me the eyeballs on her tongue. Then she'd smack her lips and say they were the best part. Horrifying.

A local reality TV show called *Road Cops* was on in the background as we ate. Some teenagers had been pulled over, their faces pixelated. The driver's big mouth sounded familiar.

'Hey, that's my car!' Mum cried.

It was Tāne's son, Wiremu, in Mum's Holden.

'This is a repeat. Haven't you seen it?' Matiu piped up. 'It was on ages ago.'

'Bloody hōhā kids,' Mum said, frowning.

'Remember when we saw Wiremu on *Crimewatch*?' I said, smirking. He'd been a grainy figure in CCTV footage of a break-in at a local pub. Mum recognised the hoodie she gave him for Christmas.

'It's not funny, girl,' Mum snapped, giving me a look and pushing her plate away.

'At least Tāne didn't get busted,' I said.

The local paper that morning reported a cache of guns, including semi-automatic weapons, had been recently stolen. We suspected Tāne's mate was the culprit, and had given him one of the guns. Since the cops hadn't found anything at Tāne's house, they had to let him go.

'Whatcha gonna do with that gun, Mum?' I said.

'E aua,' she said, and shrugged.

Tāne came over to Mum's the next day. Tall, with sweeping long dreads, pounamu tusks plugged in his earlobes and intricate tā moko spiralling across his face, arms and chest, he almost looked regal, but the princely effect was spoiled by his footwear – socks and jandals.

Bad look, bro, I thought.

'Hey Mum ... have you got that thing?' he said.

'What thing?' she said, giving him the stink eye.

Tāne managed to look sheepish and defiant at the same time.

'We've got your dope,' Mum said. 'Lucky for you the cops didn't find it!'

'Nah ... not that. Hold on to it for me. I left something in your car ...'

'I don't know what you're talking about, Tāne! Now get your black arse outside and mow my lawns!'

Tāne glowered.

'Gis my gun back!'

'Make yourself useful or fuck off home!' Mum growled. Boy, she could turn vicious. Like a pit bull.

Tāne stormed out, slamming the front door and making the whole house shudder.

'Have you been to see your girl yet?' Mum asked.

I shook my head.

'Jump in the car.'

The slow, brown river slid past like an eel under the expanse of blue sky. Waka were racing on the awa. One canoe shot ahead and kept pace with us as we drove to the urupā.

We stopped by the graves of people we knew. Admired Meha's unusual headstone, flat and portal-like. Touched Sam's faded photo. Hello Blue, old friend.

'She's not alone,' Mum said.

The oak tree at the north edge of the cemetery lay ahead. I steeled myself.

The miniature roses we planted five years ago had grown wild, obscuring the headstone. Mum clipped them back while I sat on the grave. Chunks of dark, streaky pounamu and carved black river stone had been left for her. Offerings from Tāne. It was a good spot here, under the tree and by the river.

'Which side is ours?' I said.

Mum pointed to the plot on the right. Whoever goes first will be buried deeper.

I was riding a giant golden bird when Zen Ken popped up alongside me on a mare's tail cloud. Socked feet in jandals peeked out from under his orange robes.

'Why hold on to the coffins of dead moments?' he asked, as a horde of zombies swarmed in the town below us, before whispering, 'She'll be right, mate' and striking a gong that had materialised in mid-air: BANG, BANG, BANG. It took me a minute to realise someone was pounding on the front door. I dragged myself out of bed, swearing.

A large figure loomed behind the frosted glass and I could hear the low, throbbing sound of a V8 idling outside. The shadow banged the door again, and I flung it open. A huge man with a tattoo of a skull on his cheek was standing there. He didn't look happy.

'I want my fuckin' drugs,' he said, glaring down at me. He had a gold tooth that glinted in the moonlight like a fang.

'Don't have them,' I said.

'Tāne said they are here,' he said.

'Dunno where they are!' I protested.

The truth is, I didn't. I had no idea what Mum had done with the sack of buds.

'Stop mucking me around,' he hissed.

I started to sweat.

'I – I just need to …'

'HURRY UP THEN!' he roared and kicked the door frame.

'Move out the way, girl,' I heard Mum say.

Five foot nothing in her slippers and dressing gown, Mum was standing there with the sawn-off shotgun pointed up at the chest of our visitor. He stepped back, eyes wide and hands up.

'Go get his stuff, girl. In my wardrobe.'

I did what I was told, dumping the bag at the guy's feet.

'Coming to this house in the middle of the night, making enough noise to wake the dead! I'm an old lady!' she fumed, eyes blazing. Then a flicker of recognition crossed her face.

'Hey, wait a minute …'

The man shuffled uneasily, and looked down.

'I used to teach you at the kura. Tūmanako, is that you?'

The man nodded, shamefaced.

'Āe, Whaea … it's me.'

Mum lowered the gun.

'Bloody hell!'

'Sorry to wake yous, Whaea. I didn't know this was your house.' He bowed his head.

'You used to be such a good kid at school. So bright! How's your mother?'

'She's all goods. Sorry again, Whaea.'

'Nemmind. Go home eh, it's bloody late!'

'Yes, Whaea. Geez, you're still scary. Nearly shit myself.'

Mum gave him a look.

'Aroha mai. Pō mārie,' he said, grabbing his weed and giving me a nod.

'Pō mārie, Tūmanako,' said Mum.

It was my last night in town. We were heading over to Tāne's place for a hangi. He had put it down specially. I was looking forward to a beautiful kai, but I couldn't wait to get back to the city. A week was plenty with my whānau.

'Just gotta get some gas,' said Mum. She pulled into a petrol station. A trio of patched gang members were on the forecourt, scoffing pies, leaning against a muscle car. The biggest, meanest looking one raised his eyebrows in greeting. It was Tūmanako.

'Nice Holden,' he said, and winked.

Private Dancer

I was fifteen years old, and running away. Hit the road outside Kaitaia and stuck my thumb out.

Aside from the clothes on my back (a Metallica 'Ride the Lightning' T-shirt I'd cropped myself, denim mini, cherry Docs) all I had was an army surplus bag packed with a change of clothes, a black eyeliner, and $200 from the till in my parents' shop. They weren't my real Mum and Dad anyway. He'd be happy I was gone, though he might miss having someone to blame things on. My arms still bore fingertip bruises from the big fight we had on Christmas.

'You're bloody hopeless, Joy,' he said. 'You must be a Māori.'

It did say 'Possibly Māori' on my birth certificate.

My first ride was with a pasty maths teacher who droned on about the importance of study while sneaking peeks at my legs. He dropped me off in Albany. A grazing cow gave me a baleful look. Air blurred and shimmered above the tar seal. I was hoping I wouldn't be stuck there for too long when a cream-coloured Valiant rolled up with two Black Powers in the front, two in the back. One got out to let me in. Barefoot in grimy jeans, he raised his eyebrows in greeting. My skirt rode up as I scooted over in the back seat. I pushed it down and tucked it firmly beneath my thighs. The car smelt like sweaty leather.

No big deal, I thought. *Just be cool.*

The man in the front passenger seat had a tattoo of a diamond on his Adam's apple and teeth missing. He sparked up a joint and passed it back to me.

'Are you scared, girl?'

The diamond bobbed up and down in the rear-view mirror as he side-eyed me.

I shook my head, and took a long toke.

'Nah,' I managed to say while holding in a lungful of smoke before erupting into a coughing fit.

The five of us were still laughing helplessly as we crossed the Harbour Bridge.

I had an address in Ponsonby scrawled on a scrap of paper. They took me where I wanted to go.

I crashed on the couch at a friend of a friend's villa for a week. The two hundred bucks didn't last long. I needed a job and a place to live. I had no qualifications or experience. I became a stripper. I started out dancing at the Station Hotel. The stage was a piece of wood on top of a pool table.

I climbed up on it in my heels and looked down on a crowd of long-haired, tattooed bogans. The first song I ever danced to was 'My Sharona'. I thought of my father listening to it while drinking beers in his den. It was one of his favourites. I smiled and spun around the pole.

I answered an ad looking for girls at a strip club called Stilettos on Fort Street, and was told to start on Friday. The place was black, mirrored and littered with old farm barrels also painted black. It was packed.

A chick with platinum blonde dreadlocks marched over. I'd seen her scowling on stage earlier in a Nirvana T-shirt and torn fishnets.

'You owe my flatmate money for weed,' she said. She took a long drag on a cigarette and glared at me.

'Oh yeah ... I should sort that out,' I said, looking at her through my fringe. Gina had small, bright features in a freckled face, and a shrewd intensity about her.

'You better. He owes me.' She looked me up and down, taking in my new outfit from Zambesi. Most of my earnings went on designer clothes.

'Wanna smoke a joint?' she said.

I moved into her place a week later.

'Ah fuck it, Joy,' she'd say when I'd had a bad day. 'People ... bunch a cunts.'

I lay on Ant's bed in a black lacy slip at his squat on Customs Street. He was the DJ at Stilettos, and we had started hanging out after work. We'd go to Micky Finns and get wasted. Gina didn't approve. 'Don't screw the crew,' she'd said.

'Can I give you a tattoo?' said Ant. 'I need the practice.'

'Sure.'

I was high so I didn't care. Downtown Auckland was drowning in heroin and homebake. Abandoned buildings, seedy arcades and grotty flats teemed with junkies from small towns getting strung out on smack. At least Ant's place with its wooden floors and high ceilings was relatively clean. I lay on my stomach and stared at a massive image of Aleister Crowley's face screen-printed onto fabric that Ant had hung up as a room divider. I fell asleep to the sound of his makeshift tattoo gun buzzing away. I didn't feel anything.

Hours later, I checked out Ant's handiwork in the mirrored wall at Stilettos. A shaky Grim Reaper was crudely etched across my back. I promptly stormed up to Ant and threw a drink in his face.

The manager barrelled over.

'Get out, Joy. You're fired.'

My next job was at the Love Cinema, which peddled porn movies that you could watch all day in a private booth for $25.

'Wanna watch a private movie or peep show?' I worked behind the counter at reception, and was ready to dance if requested.

The peep show was a fully mirrored room. It was quite freaky to be in there.

'I Touch Myself' by the Divinyls was blasting as I pouted in a mesh dress, taunting and teasing the sole punter lurking unseen behind the glass. I was twirling like a dancer in a music box when he burst in. The door had a lock, but I'd never used it. I felt safe in my own world, lost in the music.

He was built solidly with a neck like a bull, and stood there smirking. I knew no one would hear me if I screamed. The music was too loud.

He shoved me to the floor and pulled my legs apart. I forced myself to go limp and let my eyes roll back into my head. With a guttural cry, I threw my arms and legs around wildly underneath him with all my strength. I frothed at the mouth and let spit fly everywhere.

He jumped off me quick.

'Fuckin' freaky bitch!' he said, and took off.

I sat up in my torn dress, mussed hair and smudged make-up reflected fifty times around me. I had remembered Gina's tip to fake an epileptic fit if anyone ever tried to rape me. She always gave the best advice.

Gina started running her own peep show, so I went to work for her. 'PRIVATE DANCER' was a dark, dingy hole at the end of Gore Street and Fort, surrounded by massage parlours and nightclubs. I sat on the worn tan couch in reception, flipping through magazines as I waited for punters. I cut out a picture of Perry Farrell and taped it up next to Gwen Stefani and Chris Cornell. There was a handwritten menu tacked to the wall:

STRAIGHT PEEP $10
OPEN-WINDOW PEEP $20
SCHOOLGIRL PEEP $30
PRIVATE PEEP $40

A middle-aged Māori guy in shorts and jandals came to the entrance.

'Hi! Wanna sexy peepshow?' cooed Jess, the hot chick on reception. She had full tattooed sleeves, and every guy wanted to be with her.

His eyes scanned the menu.

'What's a straight peep?'

'You can look through the one-way mirror at our sexy dancer,' she said, and inclined her head towards me.

He glanced over and then pointed at Jess.

'Can it be you?'

Ignoring him, Jess continued with her spiel.

'Open-window peep, the window goes up, so she can see you. Schoolgirl peep, self-explanatory, and private peep you can be in the room with your own private dancer.'

He pulled out a ten-dollar note. I made a face at Jess and entered the peep show. I put on Garbage. It was either that or 'What's the Story Morning Glory' by Oasis. They'd been on repeat for the past year because we couldn't be fucked changing the CDs.

The peep show was a long, narrow room with fuchsia-pink walls, a red ceiling and black floors. There were five windows with pink curtains along one wall. A light went on over one of the windows. *Showtime.* I drew the curtains back and rocked on my heels lazily, gazing at my reflection. I would wait for tips before taking anything off. Slots for tips were above each window. They used to be below, but the punters kept putting their cocks in them.

I had just smoked a joint. It was way more fun dancing around stoned, and anyway, smoking weed made me horny. I was basically paid to masturbate all day long. I'd come two or three times some days.

Another light flicked on, so I drew back the curtains over that window too. The glass slid up to reveal a dude with long blonde hair in a Sepultura T-shirt. He locked eyes with me. I sidled over, but bills started floating down from the other window, so I went back to the first window. I backed up against it and bent over, inched my skirt down over my arse and legs, then kicked it away. I turned and blew a kiss, and started to reach around to touch myself when I saw a twenty waft down from the other guy. I crawled over.

If the tips didn't flow I'd just stand there. On good days money would come flying from all directions, raining down on my body.

I was at my flat in Parnell, a modern studio that was all white and silver. The phone rang.

'Got any weed?'

It was Gina. She was at the peep show, hanging out for a joint because she was dancing that day. I dutifully trotted down in my D&G top and Calvin Klein baggy white jeans with my papillon, Peaches. It was a crisp, sunny morning.

'Hey Joy,' said Gina and Jess in unison. I plonked down on the couch and rolled a joint, chatting away, when a punter popped his head through the door, bang on 11 a.m. opening time.

'Gotta one-on-one peep show?' he asked. Doughy and red in the face, he seemed distracted.

I shoved the joint under a copy of *The Face*.

We'll go smoke that first,' Gina whispered to me, then said out loud to the punter, 'Come back in ten minutes.'

Gina flipped the sign around on the front door to 'CLOSED', and we followed her out to the concrete alley behind our building. It smelled like wet cardboard and backed on to a Thai massage parlour. We'd often hear the girls having sex with their clients while we were smoking.

'Spark that up, Joy.'

I took a toke, and passed her the joint, when an unearthly shriek rang out.

'That's some pretty rough-sounding sex,' I said, passing the joint to Jess.

Another piercing scream.

We froze and looked at each other.

'Christ, it sounds like she's getting murdered,' Gina said.

More screaming and crying drew us out to the entrance, where we found bloodied Thai girls streaming out of the parlour on to the street.

'God, we're all just hanging by a thread,' said Jess.

I looked at Gina.

'That could have been you,' I said.

For once, she didn't have anything to say.

We finished the joint and opened the peep show for business.

Directions

It's the false dawn, that quiet, grey time before the Sun rises and the flightless spill out of their homes and go about their flightless business. We, the Crows that Shall Never Be Lost, are in our territory, the place that the flightless call Daikanyama. We roost near the station, on power lines that run in front of a stone structure full of sleeping flightless, Daikanyama Royal Copo. Their homes are stacked on top of each other, six nests deep. After a long, cold night, we flap and stretch and preen ourselves awake.

A crow says: The flightless have destroyed three of our nests.

A crow says: They are getting bold.

A crow says: We must do something.

A crow says: We must persevere with the decoy nests.

A crow says: Yes. They work for a time.

A crow says: Lay big stones in front of their densha.

A crow says: They don't like that.

A crow says: When the flightless in the green plumage comes, drive them away.

A crow says: Yes, they are green. Quite distinctive.

A crow says: They are always giving us trouble.

A crow says: Them and the ones in blue. In the black and white kuruma.

An old crow says: The ancestors told of a time when there were few flightless.

An old crow says: There was once a forest here.

An old crow says: Back then there were hawks and owls too.

An old crow says: The hawks ate our young.

An old crow says: As the flightless multiply, so do we crows.

An old crow says: Our fates are connected.

The Sun ascends.

We crows say: Greetings Ra! KĀ! KĀ! KĀ!

A hard object hurtles through the air towards us and glances off a slow, old crow. An old flightless shakes his puny talons at us. He is stooped and needs a stick to walk.

The old flightless says: You damn crows are a pest!

A crow says: You are weak and near death!

A crow says: Fuck off and die!

A crow says: We won't help you find your way when the time comes!

We all know its face. It is spotty, and its beak is the colour of squished ants and dried blood. We make sure to shit regularly around the entrance to its nest. A crow dive-bombs the flightless and rakes the top of its head with his claws. It screams and runs back into its hole, and we laugh and laugh and laugh.

The flightless call this place Tokyo. We know this because they say this often in their tinny voices, from beneath their stunted beaks. The call of Tokyo reverberates everywhere. Tokyo, Tokyo de gozaimasu.

The flightless move around on their legs but they are painfully slow. If they need to travel any distance, they travel in densha and takushī and kuruma. They also have giant birds that take them great distances across the Water. These birds aren't alive like us, but they have a kind of life. They are very canny, the flightless. The Sun made them crafty to compensate for their lack of wings. We must watch and listen to them carefully, because they tear down our nests. They hate us, but they shouldn't, because they need our help with directions later.

* * *

A crow stirs from a dream of a ruined city. In the dream, Ra was high, but barely visible through thick, grimy haze. It was twilight in the middle of the day, which confused us as it was time to eat, not sleep. We crows were ravenous, but ferocious heat made our thoughts jagged and our wings heavy. We'd dragged ourselves through churning orange skies to each of our usual foraging spots, and discovered each and every one was barren. Even Makudonarudo, usually heaped with piles of food, had been picked clean. The fountains in Yoyogi Park were bone dry. There were no flightless to be seen.

The crow furiously shakes his head to erase the stagnant memory of the dream that threatens to linger and keep him in a foul mood all day.

'KĀ!' he calls.

His mate tilts her head to eyeball him. The cherry blossoms are in full bloom, and she's feeling broody. It's time to build a nest. The pair take off and soar over the rooftops towards their chosen spot, high on a transformer, close to Daikanyama station. They search for suitable nesting material. The crow finds a pile of hangers discarded in a yard. They stockpile several, and work on entwining them together with long strips torn from fibre-optic cables.

It will take them several weeks to build the nest, for what will be their first brood.

*** * * ***

A crow sits on a clutch of three turquoise eggs speckled with grey. For eighteen days she incubates them. We, the Crows that Shall Never Be Lost, take turns to feed her. On the nineteenth day, the babies hatch. They shriek for food, their gaping mouths bottomless pits of need.

Fortunately, food is plentiful in Tokyo. The flightless leave it in piles outside their homes, covered in the Stuff That is Everywhere, in a pliant form that is no match for our strong beaks and talons. We rip these membranes open and feast on their leftovers. There is so much of it. We wonder why they don't eat it themselves. There are plenty of hungry flightless, outcast from their flock, who live under the trees in Yoyogi Park in much smaller, softer nests. More join their number by the day. Some of them talk to us and share their bread. There is one that always calls 'Ohayō!' which means 'Hello, Sun!'

In the old times, the flightless said we came from the Sun. They saw us flying high, with our black plumage, and thought we had materialised from sunspots. How do we know this? We know things. And, of course, we know that everything comes from the Sun. Our ancestors told us.

Kōhine

* * *

A crow says: It's time.

A crow says: Yes, it's time to leave the nest.

A crow says: Don't be frightened.

A crow says: It's easy.

A young crow says: Flying is the best.

An old crow says: We've all had to learn to fend for ourselves.

A crow says: We will keep watch for enemies.

A crow says: We will protect you.

A crow says: We are all in this together.

The fledglings peer over the dense thicket. The first clambers up to perch on the nest's edge.

A fledgling says: If you can't fly, you will die.

A fledgling says: O brother, you are so brave to go first.

A fledgling says: We are the Crows that Shall Never Be Lost! and flaps his wings, then launches himself into the balmy September air.

Beautiful, mellifluous sounds emanate from one of the flightless, on the ground level of Daikanyama Royal Copo. We see him tap with his talons on a strange object in his house, and his tapping corresponds to pleasing tones that rise and fall in the air. It sounds wonderful; like water coursing over rocks, baby beaks cracking the shell, the rush of air during one's first flight, and other things that make our hearts beat faster.

A young crow says: This makes me feel alive.

A young crow does a double loop in the sky.

An old crow says: This makes me remember.

An old crow bows his head and cries. His mate had been pecked to death by a rival clan, the Crows who Fly Straight.

The music rises, and rises, up and up into Ra itself, then disappears.

The flightless can do wondrous things sometimes.

A crow flies to the flightless who creates these sounds and watches him sit outside in his yard. His face is smooth; his manner still. He is eating bread, and throws out a crust. A crow retrieves it, and stashes it on a rooftop for later. A crow leaves a shard of glass in the yard.

We are roosting in the trees that overlook the yards of the flightless at Daikanyama Royal Copo. We are awakened by a disturbance on the top level. A group of young flightless squawk and hop around on a balcony. One is perched on the edge. It has long shiny hair and very large eyes: much larger than those of its friends. This flightless is not from here.

A crow says: What is it doing?

A young crow says: Is it learning to fly?

An old crow says: They can't fly, you egg.

A crow says: I think the fledgling is going to try.

A crow says: Stop! If you try to fly, you will die!

The young flightless cries out.

A crow says: Maybe it is hungry. Where's its mother and father?

The young flightless stands on the edge and throws herself into the night. Her companions scream and wail.

A crow says: KĀ!

The young flightless slips out of its body lying bent on the ground and floats up, next to us.

A crow says: Why did you do that?

The young flightless says: I don't know.

A young crow says: It understands us.

The young flightless says: What should I do?

An old crow says: You must avoid the hungry ghosts.

A crow says: You are a long, long way from home.

A crow says: We will show you the way.

Lost or forgotten we shall not be.

We are Divine Messengers, Great Navigators, the Creative Principle of the Sun.

We help those who have flown off-course find their way.

We are descendants of Ra.

We are the Crows that Shall Never Be Lost.

KĀ! KĀ! KĀ!

Pepe Tuna

Astrid lugs her suitcase into the front of the house and lets her eyes take a moment to adjust. The bedroom window is in the shade of a large pūriri tree that dapples light on the wall. She catches a flash of silver in the mirror and thinks, not for the first time: Who is this old woman?

She heads down the mountain into the village to explore. It's the beginning of summer, and Devonport is in full bloom. The gardens are immaculate, the sweeping lawns lush green. Swings hang like fruit from the gnarled pōhutukawa trees that line the streets. A tyre painted white with stencilled gold stars twists in the wind; a wooden seat dangles on knotted ropes across the asphalt. Wherever there is a well-positioned bough, some kindly person has lashed a swing to it, but there are never any children playing on them. There are no brown people either, save for a rest home worker assisting an elderly Pākehā woman down the footpath.

Back at the house, Astrid brews tea in the butter-yellow kitchen, which is filled with afternoon sun. She stands at the sash window and marvels at the Victorian garden outside. Sprays of Queen Anne's lace float above old-world roses like fairy candelabras, while fat bees feed on the lavender and hollyhocks.

'Kia ora,' the woman in the doorway says. 'I'm Maia.'

Slim, in cut-off denim shorts, she has light skin, hair and eyes, but her high cheekbones and the way she enters the room identify her as Māori. Astrid offers her tea, and they sit across from each other at the solid wood table.

Astrid says she's of Samoan and German descent, and that her hair was once black. She gestures towards her fair skin and blue eyes.

'My hair was my cultural marker.' She tells Maia about how she'd gone grey overnight. 'It was the grief,' she says. 'I've stopped dying it. I've decided to embrace cronehood. I was once quite slim. I've gained weight since the 'pause, but I don't mind, because my tits are still good. I'm not interested in meeting anyone, though.' She explains how she lost the love of her life last year. David was a brilliant man, a doctor who spoke many languages and worked in the Congo. He threw himself off the highest waterfall in Brazil.

'Why did he do it?' asks Maia.

Astrid looks her in the eye directly. 'That's why I write.'

'I write to make sense of a suicide too.'

'Huh. What's your ancestry?'

Maia relays her tribal affiliations, and says that as a child she was shown a genealogy chart written by her grandfather, who was a tohunga. 'At the top was Hinenuitepō, and at the bottom, below generations upon generations that stretch back pre-New Zealand, back to Hawaiki, he'd written my name. It blew my mind at nine years old, and it still does now. How can I be a direct descendant of the Goddess of Death?'

Maia likes the way Astrid floats around in turquoise lavalavas, and her gentle manner. She messages the actor in LA who she's flirted with online for the past six years but never met. He plays villains and troubled rogues.

I'm staying in the only house on a dormant volcano.

You're a dormant volcano.

Hah.

She checks to see if she has any other messages or online validation of any kind, but there is nothing. She hasn't heard from the young boy she slept with recently, against her better judgement.

'You're literally half my age,' she'd said to him at a party.

'I'm nearly twenty-three.'

The boy messaged in a persistent campaign to seduce her until she finally relented and let him come over. He sat on her sofa while she sat on the doorstep and smoked. They talked about architecture and film. He was taller and better dressed than she remembered. She offered him a glass of wine.

'No thanks, I drank so much already.'

'And you drove here?' she said.

He stammered for a second.

'I don't care if you don't drink,' she said.

She downed the rest of the bottle by herself while he talked about the jobs he'd been booking, moving to New York, his connections there. Do you know so and so? Have you heard of such and such? No, she had not. She brushed her teeth and finally sat next to him on the couch. He kissed her quick. He smelled like expensive soap.

'Shall we close the blinds?' he said.

'Let's go in my room.'

His body was lean and hard.

'We could have been doing this the whole time,' he said.

As soon as he'd come in her mouth, he pulled his khakis on and looked at his watch.

'I'm gonna be late for dinner. I haven't seen my father in a week.'

* * *

Astrid wakes well before sunrise. She heads to the summit of the mountain, to walk the land and say hello to it. It's still dark. A massive cruise ship is berthed in the harbour. Lights bleed into the black water like oozing paint. Where are you, David? Are you anywhere? Or nowhere? She says a silent karakia.

After breakfast, she goes out again, and searches for the sculpture that commemorates the Tainui waka making landfall. On the beach she asks locals for directions, but nobody knows where it is. 'I've lived in Devonport all my life and I've never seen it,' a man says. She eventually gives up and heads back to the house.

Maia is on the verandah with her laptop, tan legs up on the railing.

'It's so beautiful around here,' Astrid says. 'So different from where I live out west. People struggle there.'

'I keep looking at the twenty-dollar note in the donation box at the front of the house,' says Maia. 'That wouldn't last five minutes in my hood.'

'A tale of two cities.'

'It's like a bubble here. It feels like nothing bad will happen.'

'Interesting, as this place is historically so fortified,' said Astrid.

Maia wakes up to birdsong and blue sky. Yet another glorious day, but there's a crackle in the air like it needs to rain. She taps out words on the verandah, and pulls her Dodgers cap low over her face. A cruise ship drifts past, heavy on the horizon. She hates the idea of going on a cruise. A floating food court, pigs eating from a trough. Tourists struggle up the hill and point at the house. They stare at her, eyes blinking in the clear, hard light. The signs dotted around the house say 'Please don't disturb the writers.'

A sunburnt man in cargo shorts strides up the verandah steps and makes her jump.

'Oh, you're writing.'

He apologises and backs down the steps.

Astrid is at the counter, grinding salt and pepper over salmon steaks.

'Cooking dinner for us, sis.'

'Lovely.'

After eating, the two women sit on the verandah with glasses of wine. Astrid speaks of star knowledge and the garuda, a giant mythical bird that is said to have flown from Tibet to the Hokianga. Maia says she's heard of a carving of it up north on a marae somewhere.

'I'm glad they put me with you,' says Maia.

'Me too, sis.'

Maia complains about men. How they project their desires on to her; how they behave as if they are entitled to her attention and her body; how they become hungry ghosts who roam the periphery of her life, online and off.

'I'm tired of fuckboys who send me dick pics and only pay lip service to this idea of actually engaging with me as a human with a brain,' she says, as her eyes drift to her blinking phone. She turns it over.

'The art of courtship is being lost,' says Astrid. 'It's a dance, and it's about energy.'

'My ex tried to sext me last week. I hadn't heard from him since he dumped me by text, for the third time, a year ago. I kept going back even though I knew I was too good for him. He controlled me with constant criticism and disapproval. He has a girlfriend. I feel so disrespected.'

A cat screeches outside and startles them both.

'That is disempowerment. Why do men harbour these attachments to you?'

'They just want to fuck me.'

'You're a goddess, and they are attracted to one facet of you and don't acknowledge the other parts.'

'He can see that I'm doing better these days. I'm manifesting good things in my life. Yet he chose to reach out on such a base level.'

Astrid regards Maia, and thinks she needs to be more careful with her whare tangata.

'I learned not to deal with men with lower energy than mine,' says Astrid, straightening her back. 'It must be at least equal or higher. When you enter into union with someone, you take on their energy. I knew a man who used to be very beautiful and talented when he was young. He got into drugs and became ugly. He took my light; he ate my mana. He criticised me. He put me down. He used sex as a reward. He was accused of an ugly crime. I was so twisted up I made excuses for him. He was a mauri cruncher. I felt like I could never leave him because he had taken an essential part of me.'

Astrid and Maia walk down to the waterfront before dinner. A yacht sails past, with the name *Just Rewards* in brush script.

They head to the local pub and order the same thing: a kid's meal of fish and chips and a Stella Artois. They sit in silence for a while and take in their sleepy surroundings. The bouncer stationed at the pub entrance hardly seems necessary.

'When you meet someone, you don't just meet *them*,' says Astrid. 'You meet all their ancestors too. Your ancestors meet their ancestors. When you take a lover, make sure they are not worthy only of you. They need to be worthy of your ancestors.'

'My great-grandmother was a healer. She would speak to the spirits at night and they would tell her who needed healing. She would go out and gather rongoā while the moon was high.'

'Acknowledge your great-grandmother. Thank her.'

'One of my earliest memories is of being at my great-grandmother's old homestead in the Hokianga. I was playing with the back door. I locked it, and as Māmā bent over to look through the keyhole on the other side, I managed to unlock it again and burst through it, knocking her to the ground. I remember my mother's worried face, dabbing at the blood on Māmā's head. It was so red against her white hair.'

Astrid takes a swig on her beer.

'You made her blood run. That's no accident.'

They discuss themes in their work, and Maia raises the notion of intergenerational trauma.

'There's that imperative to heal yourself so you don't pass it on to your children,' Maia says. 'But my child is dead. I was too late.'

* * *

It's close to midnight. Astrid calls Maia from the hallway.

'Are you awake, sis?'

Maia gets up. There are spots of colour high on each of Astrid's cheeks, and her arms flutter. She gestures for Maia to enter her room.

'Come look at this.'

A giant moth is lying motionless on Astrid's pillow. Its vivid green wings are frosted with white; it has Roswell alien eyes and looks like a scarab.

'I was reading in bed and heard the sound of wings,' says Astrid. 'I thought it was a bird. It flew in under the closed blind and was beating against the curtain, before landing here. It's a pepe tuna. A ghost moth. They live for six years as a grub, and only forty-eight hours as a moth. They can't eat because they don't have a mouth.' Astrid's eyebrows lower. 'It's a tohu. What does it mean?'

'Its front leg looks damaged.'

'I hope it didn't come in here to die,' Astrid says.

Maia turns on all the lights, and Astrid carries the pillow outside to the verandah. Maia blows on the pepe tuna gently, but it doesn't stir. Astrid nudges it gently with her finger.

'Is it dead?'

'I don't know.'

Astrid continues to prod it, until finally its legs twitch and its wings beat weakly. The pepe tuna flies off a short distance and settles on the post of the verandah. There isn't much life left in it. Its mauri is waning.

'He chose the perfect forty-eight hours to be alive,' says Maia.

Sushi Train

Auckland City at dusk. Maia glides down the pavement in a floaty dress behind Tim, who's casual in a black printed T-shirt that underlines his belly and midlife crisis. She tries linking her arm through his, but it feels awkward because their strides don't match, so she gives up. Hare Krishnas dance and chant up Queen Street. A beggar sits on the ground with a sign that says 'I NEED HELP.'

Sushi Train is only half full. They arrive and sit at the counter. Maia selects a plate of uni gunkan, a pair of loaded battleships, and turns to Tim. He is staring at his phone.

'Aren't you hungry, babe?'

'I don't really like sushi.'

'Not at all?'

'I'll just have a beer.'

'How about some edamame?' she says, offering him a bowl.

'I'm good.'

As she eats, Maia's gaze wanders and settles on a young, attractive couple sitting in a booth. His forearms are adorned with classy tattoos; her tanned skin glows under ivory silk. The man touches the woman's face and plays with her tassel earring. The woman laughs at something he says. Maia turns back to Tim and tries to catch his eye, but he is still engrossed in his phone.

'Are you working?'

'Always.'

But he looks up when a gorgeous brunette walks into the restaurant. The woman sits down, places her handbag on the counter and carefully crosses her legs.

Chrissie is immaculately groomed, with pink nails and silky dark hair that she tosses back and forth. She checks her make-up with a tiny mirror before reaching for a seaweed salad, which she picks at daintily, conscious of being looked at. A Japanese businessman is sitting next to her. He leafs through an English phrase book, and turns to Chrissie.

'Hello! Do you come here often?'

Chrissie takes her phone from her bag and stares at it. Hiro picks up his phone. He scrolls through it, looking at videos on social media of his friends back in Tokyo. They are at his favourite yakitori place.

Hiro pays and leaves. Outside, a group of businessmen spill out of a shiny new building.

'Hey Hiro! Great first day, mate. Catch you later!' says a cheery ginger-haired man, as he pumps Hiro's arm vigorously.

'See you, mate!' Hiro says, trying to match his colleague's cheeriness.

The group heads off to a nearby pub, talking and laughing. Hiro watches them walk away.

Back at his studio apartment, Hiro takes off his shoes and places them carefully by the door. The place is sparsely furnished and full of moving boxes. He takes off his tie and holds it up so it looks like a noose, before throwing it on the sofa. Various New Zealand guidebooks are scattered about. He picks up a VR game that says 'LOSE YOURSELF!' in Japanese on the cover, and puts on a VR headset.

Chrissie checks the time on her Cartier watch and pays the bill. Eyes follow her as she leaves.

Parked nearby is Chrissie's most prized possession, a jet-black custom Dodger Charger. As she eases into the cream leather interior, it occurs to her that it's impossible to be sad in this car. She blasts some Wu Tang and sings along with the chorus as she speeds down the highway.

The Dodger Charger creeps into the garage of a dark stained cedar and concrete cube in Takapuna. Everything is floor to ceiling: doors, windows, cupboards and sliding doors that open out to the top deck. Chrissie's bedroom is shades of grey and white, and has the charmlessness of a new hotel.

Slinking into lacy black lingerie, she dons a silk robe and sprays perfume on her throat. The doorbell rings.

Chrissie sits on her bed counting money, then stuffs the thick wad of notes into her night stand while listening for the shower to stop running. The sound of the water shutting off is her cue. A paunchy man in a towel enters, and she smiles widely. He turns to hang his towel on the doorknob.

A teenager in school uniform is doing schoolwork while she eats. She has striking hazel eyes, behind thick glasses. Her phone dings and she reaches for it.

> Have you finished my maths homework yet?

> I'll send it through soon. You owe me $40.

Kelly takes a selfie brandishing chopsticks and captions it: 'Sushi Time!' Scrolling through her feed, she sees her classmates at a party. A video of the most popular girl at her school twerking receives a hundred likes in just a few minutes. Kelly checks to see how many likes her selfie has. Five, and one of them is from her mother. She deletes it.

An old woman wearing a turquoise silk scarf sits at the counter. Mary smiles at everyone, but no one seems to notice. She eats her meal slowly, and savours every bite.

On the way to her car, Mary walks past a bronze statue of a Māori chief dwarfed by construction, and remembers that he used to be surrounded by fountains.

The beggar with the sign rests his chin on his chest. Mary stops to bend down and fold a ten-dollar bill into his jar.

'Kia ora,' the man says, and smiles, revealing surprisingly white teeth. They shine out of his dirty face. A crowd has gathered to watch the string quartet. They are playing 'Eleanor Rigby'. Mary closes her eyes and listens.

Mary's heart beats faster as she crosses over the Harbour Bridge. She first came to the city forty years ago. Back then, she didn't say much. She was raised by her grandparents, who only spoke Māori. She'd always get her tenses wrong when speaking English. The past became the present.

Jack, her Scottish terrier, is waiting for her at the door of her brick and tile unit. She cooks a steak and they share it. In the living room, the walls are covered in framed photographs. Mary as a young woman with flowers in her hair. Here with her husband on their wedding day. Her children when they were children.

Mary sits down in an easy chair to watch TV with a glass of wine. A sudden twinge of pain twists like a knife in her chest. She tries to get up, but collapses, and the glass of wine falls to the floor. Jack licks her face and whines.

The string quartet plays on as the young loved-up couple from the restaurant hold each other's hands and spin round and round. The beggar swigs from a whiskey bottle, and looks up at the heavens. A shooting star burns bright across the sky for a second, then fades.

Tama

He knocks on her door with the funny knock. Moss green velvet jacket, fitted black jeans, dark curls fragrant with macadamia oil. Ringed fingers hold a guitar case. The olive planes of his face, curly halo of hair. She wants to grab fistfuls of it and bite his cheeks. They embrace. Drink and smoke. He points out a taiaha in the corner, and she tells him the white feathers that adorn it are albatross. Pokes its carved tongue at him like he's the enemy.

'Giz my fuckin' land back,' she says.

He knocks over a full bottle of beer. She cleans up the mess.

In the bedroom he sparks up a joint and they melt into one. High cheekbones that mirror her own. Full lips, juicy like his. The same supple, smooth skin. Pākehā tend to be hairy. Even the women often have a light layer of fuzz on them. His body is muscular, hot to the touch.

You're a Māori Adonis.

He laughs, a free, easy laugh, often.

I like that you're Māori too, he says. I don't know why I always date Pākehā.

Same.

But she knows why she doesn't go for Māori boys. They remind her too much of her brothers. Tama, however, reminds her of herself.

You're so happy, she says.

My baseline is higher than most. I get hypermania.

You're bipolar?

Yeah. I pretty much feel high all the time.

She guides him inside her, eases down slowly, clenches her pussy.

No one's ever fucked me like this before.

You mean … properly?

You bad bitch.

They wake to watery, sullen skies. Smoke a spliff and fuck some more. He moves above her, head back and eyes closed. Hushed, languid hours.

Just a couple of randy browns, he says, laughing, and his hair falls in her face.

Coffee and cigarettes. He strums his guitar softly on her sofa, and grins when he catches her studying him. A pair of rosellas alight in the peach tree in the front yard. Green tails, yellow bellies and blue wings brighten the dreary day, like a circus in winter. They cry pink pink pink, in metallic voices.

They're us, he says.

'We should probably talk,' he says. 'My doctor said if I keep staying up late and being too hectic, it's no good for anybody.'

And then, there's a girl in his story.

You can't keep seeing her.

She's really nice though.

I don't care.

Okay. I'd rather hang out with you.

He returns bearing gifts – a handmade chocolate strawberry, floral shorts from the op shop, a tiny brass ashtray shaped like a fish. She gives him a Mexican sacred heart covered in milagros: tiny silver pistols, limbs, creatures, faces; charms fixed with nails to painted wood.

You have a lot of nice things, he says.

Wear this. She selects a finely carved bone heru from the taonga on her dresser.

He fastens his long hair into a topknot with the comb. A manaia figure stares down at her with its pāua eye.

There. You look like Māui.

He admires himself in the mirror.

Woah. I look like I have mana or something.

Be careful with it, she says.

Who's this?

Gilt-framed photo, between the Buddha she brought back from Thailand and a Huicol beaded skull.

My daughter.

He takes in the ikat silk cushions, the French bistro chairs, the paintings.

You have really good taste, he says. Your whare is an extension of you. That first weekend was like some kind of dreamy holiday.

He notices her fresh mani/pedi. Pale green for hands, peach for toes.

I like how you take care of yourself. Ooh, is this new? He strokes her sleeve: navy silk. I haven't seen you wear this before. You're really quite special, you know.

She feels like a goddess.

Her friend is suspicious. Are you sure he's not lovebombing you?

He's the happiest person I've ever known. He sings and plays the guitar every morning.

God, doesn't that get annoying? says the friend.

He's very talented.

Being with him is like having her face turned to the sun.

My ex was a nasty piece of work, he says. She talked shit about people.

You're talking shit about her.

She dumped me because her friends didn't like me.

How could anyone not like you? You're so likeable. They must be arseholes.

Miserable people tend to really hate me.

He has no money for cigarettes, so she buys him some.

Can you get a pouch of tobacco instead of cigarettes?

It's too expensive, she says. Why are Māoris so bad with money?

Because we never had it, he says.

Should I wear these?

A hand at her ear.

Hoops shaped like fucking gold cobras, he says. Hell yes.

He wears a black shirt with lilies and a peacock-shaped ring with sapphire eyes.

Māori power couple, he says.

Her writer friends troop through the door and shed their winter coats; click their fingers to his soul playlist.

She introduces him, eyes shining, huge smile banana'd across her face.

Wow. You two look like a star couple.

Wine and conversation. A joint is passed around.

Who's hungry? he says, and serves pork belly sliders, haloumi for the vegetarian, two kinds of dumplings.

This food is great, Tama.

He's an excellent chef.

Out comes the guitar. A powerful, rich baritone unfurls from his chest, fills the room. She takes photos and notices his laughter between songs is a little brittle; there's something hard in the eyes.

Everyone claps, impressed.

Phenomenal. Really great. Man of many talents.

The writers read from their work in turn. Tama rolls his eyes and groans throughout.

What the fuck? she mouths.

I'm bored! he declares in a stage whisper, and continues to make faces.

She can't concentrate on the words. Finally, she pulls him aside.

Don't be so rude to my guests.

He scoffs.

The problem with most people is they can't take criticism.

Are you serious?

They rejoin the others.

I'm sorry. I can't believe he did that.

Her friends brush it off, but her mood has soured. They hang out and drink for another hour, then everyone leaves except for Tama's friend, who arrived late and missed the reading.

Why would you disrespect my friends like that? You ruined my party.

You embarrassed me, he says.

I don't even know who you are right now.

His friend tries to defend him.

Who the fuck are you? she says.

The friend leaves.

Tears stream down Tama's face. He rocks back and forth on his heels and hugs himself, almost hysterical.

I've had enough grief in my life, she says. I don't need this. She leaves the room. He follows her and cries while she gets into bed, pulls the covers over her head.

Oh, *I* know what it's like to lose a daughter, he says.

She tenses. Sits up.

Huh?

I said I lost a daughter too.

What are you talking about? If you really wanted to see your daughter, you could. I can't. I'll never see my girl again. It's not the same.

No, no, no, I know what it's like.

Are you seriously trying to argue with me about this?

I lost a daughter too.

My daughter is dead you cunt.

She gets out of bed, hits him in the face swiftly, three times.

Ow, he says. Not the face.

What is she doing? She steps back. He's beside himself. Roars off in his car. Minutes later, a thud at her door. Plastic shopping bag on the step, tatty and crumpled. Inside is the heart she gave him, and the heru, in pieces.

The Actor

I went out for smokes and ended up with a tranny.

> *Are you drinking again? Your LA
> people won't like that.*

I haven't heard from my agent in six months.
She's friends with the girl.
And the girl isn't speaking to me.

> *Again? That sucks. Being ignored is the worst.*

I'm done with the pleading and horseshit.
She'll look for me in every man she sees.

> *Her loss.*

I have this theory. If women would let me pull their heads into my chest, and just relax, for a second, and stop with all the fucking crazy.

> *I want someone to pull my head into their chest!*
> *And to watch TV with.*

When it turns to shit with the boyfriend, ask me to hold you ... You're still the best thing, even though you need my money.

> *I didn't ask you for money.*

What did you ask for?

> *Nothing.*

Well, that's easy. I have a ton of that.

He didn't know how long they'd been talking. A few years now – six, seven? He'd stumbled across her profile through a mutual friend and liked her face. They'd go for long periods without any contact, and then he'd reach out after a relapse, a break-up, a lonely spell. It was late September, and he was drowning in all three.

He woke with a ragged gasp, and gripped the sides of the black claw-foot bathtub. Tepid water sloshed on to the tiles as he hauled himself out. He looked at his reflection. Why had he hung out with that idiot neighbour for two days? He thought back. He'd been in the hallway clutching a beer and about to enter his apartment, when Dan had sidled up behind him and said, 'Hey buddy, wanna go to the bar?' Of course that led to more beer, shots of tequila and Dan cock-blocking him when he'd tried to talk to the one interesting girl in the bar, and then coke later at Dan's place, where Dan had regurgitated the same tired old stories he'd heard last time, and the time before that.

Are you okay? Just checking in.

Fair. Coke booze run.

Are you mid- or post-bender?

Vodka comedown. I yelled at Dan for two days.

The neighbour/stalker? That doesn't sound pleasant.

He kept asking me if I was depressed. I said I'm not depressed, I'm morose.

Lol.

Not sure why I'm such a maniac. Threatened to smash his thick head in. Loud. In front of his lady.

> Hahaha.

I'm a cunt. Mean.

> Yeah, I can see that. I can be pretty mean too.
> It's kind of fun.

He just triggers my shit.

> Are you high now?

A bit.

> I want to be doing coke with you.
> You could yell at me.

I keep thinking I have a hat on. I don't.

> That's hilarious.

I'm calling you.

> Do you want to talk to me?

Yes.

> One sec. I have to put some pants on.

It always seemed to be sunny on her side of the world. All beachy hair and tanned limbs, she'd leap up to refill her wine glass and he'd eyeball her ass in faded Daisy Dukes. She laughed at his jokes, chin on hand, wide smile.

Winter had descended on Toronto. There would be months of gloom. He wore a navy fishermen's beanie and tartan scarf, and puffed away on a pipe.

'You look like an old-timey sailor. A man of the sea. A seaman.'

'Semen.'

'You're obsessed with bodily fluids.'

'I'm drunk.'

'Are you?'

'A bit.'

'Where are you?'

'At home. Hair of dog issue.'

'I see.'

'I adore you. I want to come there. Life is short and you're an idiot. Show me around.'

'People always say life is short, when actually it's really long.'

'I want to meet you. Bucket list.'

'Fuck it list.'

He felt calm after talking to her. She didn't judge when he fell off the wagon after months of sobriety and a stint in rehab. Wasn't fazed when he told her about the time he drank a bottle of sherry at Christmas and lunged at his own mother across the dinner table. She had her own problems, liked a drink too, and understood that he used the booze to quell the voices. To drown out the shitty committee.

I'm at the London Hotel, LA. Fancy as fuck.

Ooh, nice! I hope you're lying out by the pool.

Ten minutes from my ex.

Uh oh. Have you heard from her?

I sent flowers a week ago. Gave my schedule.

And nada?

Nada.

Are you drunk?

I'm not sure.

That means yes. What time is it there?

11. Walked the Strip and ran into some old chums who further eroded my faith in humanity.

You didn't hang out?

For a beer, until the hustle became unbearable. Empty LA. I have a project. I'm smoking a cigar. I'm someone. I'd lick your asshole right now.

Woah. Well, I've just showered so you're good to go.

Random filth. Because you're kind.

You say the sweetest things.

It was in a loving way. If it turned you on, so be it.

Mildly.

He fixed a drink from the minibar, jerked off and went to sleep. The next morning, he drank a beer while he packed, ordered an Uber and then, en route to the airport, left a postcard on his ex's car.

Like a stalker?

It was an F. Scott Fitzgerald quote.

You need to move on.

People always make it sound so easy.
Just move on, don't think about her, be happy. I won't fall in love again because of the platitudes.

I get it. You remember how I was over the boy.
He blocked me and it fucking sucked.

This whole cutting people off, the way people just block now. If you don't want me and it's done, I get it, but say it to my fucking face. Release me.

He thought about the girl. The quiet times they'd had together at his place. They didn't go out much. She did her yoga, while he painted or read scripts. He liked having someone to cook for; he'd been a chef before the acting.

The endless ruminations over the trip to Europe. The good part, before they'd fought over his drinking. If he'd known it would all turn to shit, he would've clung to the coat-tails of each golden moment and begged them to stay. He pored over the photo album she'd made for him. Pages and pages of Polaroids, carefully selected and affixed and sweetly captioned. It must have taken her weeks. Here they are, wearing woolly hats and laughing at some joke. Here is the proof. She loved me. The curve of her dancer's leg. Zero body fat. Her drive. Her hustle. Her ambition. He had to respect that, though he felt used. He'd been young and hungry once. The light in her amber-ringed eyes when things were still good between them. He admired her resolve in not speaking to him, even though it was dumb. There was a nobility to it.

> *I'd always think it would be so much better if the boy was here, and it would make me crazy that he was spending summer with someone else. I feel good today though.*

I can't even imagine the girl with someone else.
It would make me sick.

The Actor

It's not pleasant. Gutting he came over twice this week and snuck back home to the girlfriend in the early hours.

Yes ... I couldn't do it.

I realised I couldn't.

She talked of some kind of friendship. That just seems painful to me. I want it and I hate it.

So did he. Lasted less than a week.

I'm too faulty to love or trust fully.

That's not true.

I was very mean with words.

My ex-husband said terrible things to me when he was drunk, and I never forgot them.
Fat old bitch.
I can do much better than you.

Rude drunken words are rarely to be taken personally. That's just the drink talking.

Everything mindless hurts.

Yes.

Maybe we knew each other in a past life.

I think a future life.

He'd brought up meeting her in real life several times now, but she always found a reason to postpone. He offered to fly her to Canada in December. They discussed meeting either in Tokyo or LA in March, but made no concrete plans. This, whatever it was, was safe for her. Also, she wouldn't stop selling herself short to morons.

Guess who's here.

Uh oh. September fourteenth.

Hah. Yes. It's funny you two have the same birthday.

Sexy time. I wish my ex was here. Though it's best I stay away from the women folk. Like land mines ... you step on one ... then you're stuck until you choose to move and be blown to pieces.

No sexy time.
We took some MDMA and he fell asleep.
Wtf.
Boring.

I might take some mushrooms.

Do it. It's your job to entertain me, since he's passed out.

He'd recently begun micro-dosing. The relief from his depression had been instantaneous, a miracle. The dosage had crept up, though. Instead of achieving just an elevated mood, he'd been mildly tripping out most days. He'd have to be careful. Right now he felt wooo.

On video chat, she led him outside to her yard – white picket fence, still light out there – then put her phone into the interior of a tree. Trunk and tangle of branches.

'Listen to that! Song thrushes.'

'They are exceedingly chirpy.'

'Like me. I'm rolling. High as fuck.'

'Me too.'

Then September fourteenth appeared on the periphery, bleary eyed and sceptical, and she had to go.

* * *

Well, that didn't last long. After he gets his 'me' fix he goes back to the gf and all his couple shit. Of course he winds up telling me that he is happy after all, loves the gf and won't leave. I'm such a fool for believing his 'I miss you, I made the wrong choice' bullshit, especially after he lied about her in the first place. He caught me at a weak moment. Sorry to dump on you.

That's okay.

I want to live in a lighthouse. Or a cave.

I'm a lighthouse.

> Ha yes. You are. Don't let me crash on the rocks.
> A beacon of hope.

You're beautiful.

> Bracing myself for an insult.

And not super dumb.

> Just super foolish. Clever ain't wise.

You're special. It's okay.

> Thanks.

I just got 'Weren't you famous a while ago?'

> Lol. From who?

Liquor store.

> Oh. Haha.

Then bought a woman's groceries because she looked sad.

> That's sweet. Would have made her day.

He sent four Spotify links.

> *You already sent me those last two. How many chicks are you sending songs to?*

All the ones with pussies.

> *One of my guy friends messaged me. 'Have your boobs grown?' I said 'No. Have yours?'*

Ha. They do look quite enormous in that pic.

> *Must be the angle.*

He woke up the next morning exhausted. Heart and limbs heavy, mind racing. Pot pills or mushrooms? Both? The mushrooms had lost their efficacy, and his relatively stable mood had plateaued, then crashed.

He fixed himself some gruel, which technically wasn't gruel, but his own concoction of whatever cereal he had on hand and fruit and healthy powders and shit. He ate it standing. The day stretched ahead of him. What had formerly cheered him – gym, fishing, a ride on the bike, painting – now seemed pointless. He'd have to leave the apartment. He threw a trench coat over the sweats he'd slept in and made a dash down the street for supplies. It was drizzling, but he barely noticed. Safely back home, he disappeared into a bottle of whiskey.

* * *

The chats came to an abrupt halt. It felt strange not connecting. He left the apartment on a pub crawl for one, headphones in, to be in the world but not engage with it. At the bar he watched a young couple in the corner. The woman looked upset; the man indignant, then ashamed. 'Whiskey please, bartender. Neat.'

Blackout.

Days later he was somehow at the airport. 'Tis the season to be jolly. Going home for Christmas. Plenty of old people's drinks there. Port and sherry.

Waking from a binge is not fun.

Oh dear.

How long was the binge?

Ten days I think.

That's a long time. Are you at your parents' place?

Yes.
Rehab.
With pets and home cooking.

Well, you're in the right place. Just relax. Be taken care of and get better.

I've been off my head.

I know. Try not to get anxious about that.

The Actor

Have I been crazy? You can tell me.

>*I haven't talked to you recently. Though the past couple of times you were pretty wasted. But still lucid.*

Okay ... cool.

>*You told me about Dan and all that drama, the burst pipe, getting your paintings back.*

Was having a psychotic break a little.

>*I didn't think you were crazy. You seem fine mid-blackout.*

Last three days I could see the skeletons of cats.
And when I closed my eyes, Mexican radio.

>*That's frightening. Time to get back on the wagon.*

Soul hurts.

>*That's a yuck feeling. You're a good person. Be kind to yourself.*

I know, but a drunk asshole when hurt.

>*You're not drunk now. Leave it in the past.*

Yes.

Christmas, for Christ's sake. Pull this cracker, don a paper hat, play a dinky wind-up Santa game. Haggis and oatcakes. Scrabble with his parents, Scottish records from his childhood playing. His folks were sweet and kind and doted on him. He was a boy again. Swaddled and soothed. He read a book about the Stoics. He didn't drink. After three weeks of this he felt okay. On an even keel, out of the doldrums, back on course, land in sight. Almost cheerful. He packed up a rental with childhood mementos and the rescue puppy his mother had found him, and made the ten-hour drive over the mountains back home. The dog whined and shivered in the back. Who knows what the previous owners had done to her. Those shitheads. He'd take care of her. They'd go for walks and dance every day, and he'd teach her how to play dead for treats. She would fix him.

She sent a selfie with a hibiscus flower tucked behind her ear.

    Hi pretty face.

In the islands, if you put it behind your left ear, you're available.

You're unavailable.

Lol.

The Actor

If it's in your ass crack?

Well, no one will see it there. What did you do today?

Mushroom ceremony.
85 percent horseshit.
Four hours. It was three hours too long.

Where was it? Who did it? Did you trip out?

Not enough. A dude's apartment.

Lame.

You good?

Was hanging out with my best friend before. We are both depressed about our love lives. And you?

Semi-drunk.

Are you drinking with friends? You're such a social butterfly these days.

Social moth. Just Paul. Booze is part of his process.

Oh cool. Have fun.

He has a great life. I feel like a skid.

I hear ya. I often feel that way.

But I'm a hot electric disaster.

I'm just a disaster.

It was true; he had been around people a lot lately. Back home, alone, he struggled. The first morning at the dog park, the dog wouldn't come when called, but would happily run up to strangers. 'Who feeds you?' he demanded, back at the apartment. 'Look at all this nice food and treats and blankets.' She retreated to her crate and refused to come out. He'd slid off the wagon again. He hadn't wanted to drink, but that's how Paul rolled when he was writing, and it had been fun working on the script and shooting the shit with him.

Why did the dog hate him? Perhaps he had a demon that came out when he was in a blackout. Dogs would sense shit like that. Years ago, a woman with Pre-Raphaelite hair, some kind of healer, had said there was a dark entity dwelling within him.

He went to the liquor store.

I'm feeling done.

Done with what?

Life.

Why?

The Actor

Tired of the agreement. I'll work until sixty.
Then I'm done.

> *What? You're gonna kill yourself when you turn sixty?*

I hate it here.

> *You hate Toronto?*

Being human. Lack of interest.

> *You were good at your parents' place.*

I pretend.

> *Faking it until you make it kinda works though.*

I'm done. Can't turn it around.

> *You can always turn it around.*

No.

> *What's triggered this?*

I'm too smart or too dumb to go on.

> *This will pass, you know.*

Platitudes will keep me warm.

> *It's not a platitude. Life is in constant flux, everything always changes, your mental state is not fixed.*

I'll walk the earth like a dying robot. I'll do and say what's expected.

> *I wonder why you get like this.*

I don't belong.

> *Well, join the club.*

* * *

> *How are you?*

Heavy. But alive.

> *That's good.*

You're important.

> *I'm often on the verge of tears.*

Come here. I mean, it's okay. But come here. Bring your dog.

> *Lol. We can be dog people. I can't right now though.*

I'll pay your way. Not for sex.

> *I know.*

The Actor

I need someone to cook for.

> *I wanna be cooked for.*

I walked the dog to the ocean. Forgot it was beautiful there because inside my head there's a dumpster fire.

> *Being next to a body of water is healing.*

I'm in the bath writing sad poetry.

> *Man, this Corona shit. Drives me crazy when people don't take it seriously. My friend said yesterday more people die from the flu. Uh, no they don't. It's ten times deadlier.*

If the internet got a virus, we would all perish.

> *Ha yep. I told you about when I left my body right?*

We both like doing that.

> *An out-of-body experience. After a dark night of the soul.*

Yes.

> *I was stone cold sober and it was real.*

Same.

> *All my grief was gone.*

Peace briefly. And the world crept back in with its labels and objects.

Lockdown days were formless, but he was built for robust isolation. Simple routines. He ate gruel, canned tuna, Cobb salad. No hot meals. Some days he felt okay. Others he didn't. He painted. He smoked. He took long baths. He watched documentaries. He meditated. He had bouts of sobbing. He didn't drink.

> *I better get up. I slept in today.*
> *The dog doesn't want to get up either.*

I better shave my balls.

> *Ha. What for?*

Exactly.

> *Futile ball shaving.*

Put that on my tombstone. Death would be an interesting change of pace.

> *I don't want you to die.*

I won't.
I'm curious about the sad decay. And I've yet to
be happy.

> *Ever?*

Sista

Hellooo bud. How you travelling, sis? Yes, I went and fkn died, bud. Wtf. He gone, lol. NO GOOD. Probably hear from you more now, you bloody bitch! Dad's here. Just the bloody same bud. Still smokes like a chimney. That shit'll kill him lol. Too late. Aria is all good! She says don't worry about her. Also said you need to do something about your waka-blonde hair. Lol. She's got a big waha just like her mother. What's she like? Like THAT, bud! NO GOOD! She's such a crack-up. She told me that when she was little, round at Mum's, she goes to you 'How come when Uncle

Jase comes out of the shower, he wears his towel around his chest, and not his waist?' No, I don't have any tits bub, lol.

It's not too bad here, actually. I feel bad for Mum though. Give her a hug from me, will you? Poor thing. First Dad, and now me. Can't wait for you to get here. But not too soon, eh bud!

Did you get the butterflies I sent you, bud? Saw you being a tangiweto at the park. That Anita Baker song got you eh. We used to love that one. Ahhh! Shut up, bud, you can't sing lol. Kalofae! Loving the playlist that you made. All our old favourites. Rhythm & Black, bud, OH GOOD.

Lucky we caught up in Sydney before I kicked the bucket … bit fkn sudden. It just goes to show, bud, everyone is just hanging by a thread. Do everything you want to do, bud. Live your dreams and all that shiz! Fuck around! If I was you, I'd just walk around in my undies, lol.

Okay my darling budness, I have to go. Love you to the moon and back my sis.
    FA!

Leaping-off Place II

You always wanted to fly. Remember that time you went hang-gliding? As you ran off the mountain as fast as you could, your legs circling wildly in mid-air like a cartoon character, it occurred to you, *hey, if I crash I could die,* but it was too late. You were airborne. A pocket of warm air bore your paper plane up and you drifted in it, above a pair of hawks that were coasting along in it too, playing with the currents. They made having fun look majestic. You never thought you'd have a bird's-eye view of birds flying, and you wished you could take a picture of them and look at it whenever you wanted to feel free.

All your life you had recurring dreams of flight. Instead of arms outstretched in front of you, superhero style, you would stand upright with knees slightly bent, arms doing a reverse doggy paddle at your sides. As you rose through the viscous air backwards, you looked over your shoulder so as not to collide with anything. When you flew indoors, two times out of three, your arse would get stuck in the upper corners of rooms.

Now you hover untethered in the curdled sky poisoned pink by the Eastern Capital, far, far away from your homeland. You see everyone in that city that knew you and you hear what they are thinking. Their regrets and judgements, their speculations and pity, their pain and their aroha. You turn away from the life you had there. You are not of that place and of those people. You learned their ways and their language, and some loved you and you them, but you were always an outside person. You never knew that until someone called you that. You thought you were just living your life in the world, but you had to admit that cunt was right.

Pluck a spray of plum blossom and tuck it into your obi shot through with golden threads. Brace yourself as an invisible cord of braided flax unfurls from your solar plexus and draws you west, towards Rā, dissolving ever so slowly into the sea like a drop of honey. Skim across the Great Ocean of Kiwa as a flying fish, and from time to time delicately brush against the surface, disrupting the tessellations of light that ripple across it. You pass over the mountains of Raiatea, and a fragrance wafts up from a garden of ever-blooming flowers. It smells like white blossoms at night and lovers dressed in black. The scent is so bewitching you wish to stay a while, but you must press on.

You notice the direction of the current hitting the prow of your waka has changed, indicating land. Birds circle in the distance. Use the cosmic marks on your hand like a sextant and adjust course.

You're home. Your family is gathered by the Whanganui River. It's a bit embarrassing, the open casket. It took a while to get your body back, but Nana insisted you be seen.

They shut the door on your bloated face and bury you. You tell them not to cry, but they don't listen.

They'll be okay. They'll follow you soon enough.

You fly up the river, over Rānana and Jerusalem. You coast over Pīhanga the lady mountain and the Great Cloak of Tia. You speed up over Tāmaki Makaurau and slow down over the Hokianga. Voices summon you in Māori, which you don't speak, but you can understand them, and you reply in Japanese and they can understand you. Instead of 'āe', you say 'hai'. Instead of 'ahi', you say 'hi'. Instead of 'awa', you say 'kawa'. And instead of 'hime', they say 'hine'.

Kōhine

Finally, you are here, at the Tail End of the Fish. There is a lighthouse. A nuclear family poses for a photograph in front of the famous yellow signpost with the signs that point in all directions. EQUATOR 3827 km. TROPIC OF CAPRICORN 1220 km. TOKYO 8475 km. You stand next to the children and flash a V sign. The mother and father puzzle over the orbs of light that appear in the picture.

Seagulls keen and the restless surf smashes the jagged cliffs. The wind whistles like the devils do at night. Walk the broken ridge to a pōhutukawa tree starred with red, Te Pua o te Rēinga. Retrieve the plum blossom from your waist and leave it as a token of your passage at the base of the great tree. Climb the wizened roots and cling on to a bough for dear life. Swing yourself out, one arm at a time, like you are on the monkey bars at kindergarten, until you hang over the churning ocean, legs kicking the air.

Now, let go.

Acknowledgements

I couldn't have written these stories and completed this book without incredible guidance and support from: Steve Braunias, Daisy Coles, Eboni Waitere, Bryony Walker, Te Kani Price and the team at Huia Publishers, the Māori Literature Trust, John Cranna, Callum Keith Rennie, James George, Michelle Koizumi, Ian Messer, my Te Papa Tupu whānau: Nadine Anne Hura, Cassie Hart, Shilo Kino, Ataria Sharman and Hone Rata; Amy McDaid, Rosetta Allan, Ruby Porter, Shayne Carter, Hayden Fritchley, Kate Brebner, Jarad Bryant, Ava Williams, The Surrey Hotel Grey Lynn, the Michael King Writers' Centre, and the Dan Davin Literary Foundation.

Much love to all my dear friends and whānau around the world, for being a part of our journey, my beloved Monique and I, from Aotearoa to Japan and back again.

Ka nui te mihi ki tōku māmā a Ihapera Te Wake me tōku pāpā a Michael Lenihan.

Jason Jackson Ohlson, I love and miss you, my bud. See you on the other side.